APPIUS AND VIRGINIA

Books by G.E. Trevelyan:

Appius and Virginia – 1932
Hot-House - 1933
As It Was in the Beginning - 1934
War Without a Hero - 1935
Two Thousand Million Man-Power - 1937
Theme with Variations - 1938
William's Wife - 1938
Trance by Appointment - 1939

APPIUS
AND
VIRGINIA

G.E. Trevelyan

Published in 2020
by Abandoned Bookshop
Imprint of EyeStorm Media
312 Uxbridge Road
Rickmansworth
Hertfordshire
WD3 8YL

abandonedbookshop.com

First published by Martin Secker in 1932
'The Eclipse of G.E. Trevelyan' copyright © 2020 by Brad Bigelow

Cover by Nell Wood: nellwood.co.uk
Cover photograph by Pat Whelan

British Library Cataloguing in Publication Data
A catalogue record for this book is available from the British Library.

Printed by CPI Group (UK) Ltd, Croydon CR0 4YY

ISBN: 9781785632181

The Eclipse of G.E. Trevelyan

Gertrude Eileen Trevelyan's life is a cautionary tale. She may have come closer than any writer of her time to fulfilling Virginia Woolf's vision from *A Room of One's Own*. Give a talented young woman writer 'a room of her own and five hundred a year, let her speak her mind and leave out half that she now puts in,' Woolf predicted, 'and she will write a better book one of these days. She will be a poet.' In Trevelyan's case, she found her room at 107 Lansdowne Road in Kensington in 1931, had five hundred a year thanks to her father's modest fortune, and put the two to good use, producing eight novels of striking originality in the space of nine years. She had a small circle of friends, avoided the limelight, reviewed no books, neither taught nor edited, made no trips abroad or otherwise diverted her time and energy from the task of writing. This allowed her to take great risks in style, structure and approach, to create works of imaginative intensity unequalled by any novelist of her time aside from Woolf herself. Then a German bomb hit her flat and she and her books were forgotten.

Ironically, Trevelyan's career began with worldwide publicity. 'First Woman Winner of Newdigate Prize' announced a headline in *The Times* of Wednesday, June 8, 1927. In her last year as an undergraduate at Lady Margaret Hall, Oxford, Trevelyan won the Newdigate Prize for English verse. Although the prize amounted to a mere £21, the novelty of its award to a woman led papers throughout the English-speaking world—from Kenosha, Wisconsin to Auckland, New Zealand—to print the story with similar headlines in the following weeks. When she died in early 1941, most of the few papers that printed an obituary cited the Newdigate Prize as her primary achievement.

The actual presentation of her award, at the Oxford Encaenia on July 1, 1927, proved anticlimactic. For the first time in its history the ceremony had been shifted one day later to allow participants to witness the first total eclipse of the sun visible in England since 1724. Most took the opportunity to leave Oxford early. Trevelyan's award was the last to be presented, coming after dignitaries including Field Marshal Ferdinand Foch and Field Marshal Viscount Allenby were awarded honorary degrees. Her win was seen as a symbolic victory for women at Oxford. 'This,' *The Oxford Times* concluded, 'doubtless, explained the presence in the gallery of many undergraduettes in their quaint hats.' Trevelyan's poem 'Julia, Daughter of Claudius' was quickly forgotten. Basil Blackwell printed five hundred copies and a handful of reviews appeared. The *Daily Mail*, while noting that 'many winners of the Newdigate Prize have subsequently lapsed into obscurity', predicted that 'Miss Trevelyan's future work will be watched with interest'.

Many of the articles about Trevelyan's prize drew attention

to her family connections. It was true, as stated, that she was related to the historian George Macaulay Trevelyan and a line of baronets and cabinet ministers. These were not close relations, however. Her grandfather—the historian's great uncle—was a vicar who had been removed after speaking out against Church reforms and spent the rest of his life as a 'priest without care of souls'. Her father's career was even less distinguished. Having inherited a comfortable legacy, Edward Trevelyan spent his time riding and managing his garden. He married in his forties; Gertrude, born in Bath in 1903, was his parents' only child. She remained close to them all her life.

There was also nothing exceptional about Gertrude Trevelyan's childhood. She attended the Princess Helena College in Ealing as a boarder, winning the school's essay prize two years in a row but graduating without distinction. She went up to Oxford without a scholarship, entering Lady Margaret Hall in the autumn of 1923. Of her time at Oxford, she once wrote, 'Did not: play hockey, act, row, take part in debates, political or literary, contribute to the Isis or attend cocoa parties, herein failing to conform to the social standards commonly required of women students.' She was thereby able to maintain 'a position of total obscurity'. After Oxford, Trevelyan did little of note at first. She published a few poems and wrote some forgettable articles for minor magazines. She lived in a series of women's hotels, then moved to the flat in Kensington in 1931. And here, Gertrude Trevelyan's biography effectively stops. Until her death in 1941, there is almost no record of her life outside the reviews of her novels.

The unremarkable facts of Trevelyan's life offer a stark contrast to the originality and intensity of her novels—none more powerfully than her first novel, *Appius and Virginia* (1932). Its story is novel enough: a 40-year-old spinster buys an infant orangutan and takes him to a cottage in a remote country village where, for the next eight years, she attempts to raise him as a human. Some compared the book to John Collier's 1930 novel, *His Monkey Wife*, in which a schoolteacher marries a literate chimpanzee.

Phyllis Bentley, writing in the *New Statesman*, felt that *Appius* 'emerges triumphantly from the comparison.' She found Appius a tragic figure. 'One lays down the book grieving oddly over this half-man and feeling that in some sense he is symbolic of human destinies.' Bentley understood that this book was much more than a bit of exotic novelty. Trevelyan's aim, in fact, was broader: to reveal the impossibility of genuine communication and understanding between two beings, whether of the same species or not.

Her aim was so ambitious that many of her reviewers failed to grasp it. In the *Daily Mail*, the veteran James Agate dismissed the book as 'pretentious puling twaddle...saved from being disgusting only by its frantic silliness.' *The Sketch* found it 'absorbing but horrible, and almost entirely devoid of beauty.' American reviewers tended to take the book literally: 'an absorbing study in the education and environmental adjustments of a young ape,' said the *New York Times*.

On the other hand, Gerald Gould, then one of England's most influential critics, was in awe of Trevelyan's accomplishment: 'So original is it, indeed, that I have scruples about writing the word "novel" at all.' Instead, he argued, 'one must feel grateful to anybody with a sufficiently strong mind to break such new ground.' Gould chided those who would be put off by the eccentricity of the book's premise: 'One reads a story for the story,' he wrote; 'if it makes its own world, and compels our judgment inside, that is all we have the right or reason to ask. In this difficult and surprising task,' he concluded, 'the author succeeds.'

Leonora Eyles, who remained Trevelyan's most steadfast supporter among critics, applauded the novelist's ambition. 'It must have required considerable courage to conceive *Appius and Virginia* and to carry out the conception so carefully,' she wrote in the *Times Literary Supplement*. She warned, however, that 'Miss G.E. Trevelyan demands equal courage from her readers.' Eyles recognised how the nature of the relationship between Virginia and Appius shifts in the course of the story: 'So by degrees she forgets his subhuman origin and her own scientific project and demands of him the affection of a son.' For Eyles, though, Appius's lot remains throughout that of a victim, meekly accepting what he understands only as 'incomprehensible and indigestible scraps of information from his loving torturer.' Indeed, some today will find *Appius and Virginia* a prescient account of the perils inherent in playing with the boundaries between humans and the animal world.

Trevelyan's second novel, *Hot-House* (1933), draws upon her time at Oxford. *Hot-House* is a clinical dissection of the organism of a women's college, focusing on its deleterious effects on an impressionable undergraduate, Mina Cooke. Mina tries to gain attention through exaggerated mannerisms, but she fools herself more than her classmates, blowing the casual courtesy of instructors into romances of operatic proportion. Trevelyan succeeds perhaps too well into taking us into the mind of a ruminator, filling too many pages with Mina's broodings over a glance, a misunderstood invitation, a suspected slight. On the other hand, *Hot-House* amply demonstrates the extent to which Trevelyan committed to her fictional experiments. If in this case the experiment proved less than successful, it was not because she approached her task half-heartedly.

Her third novel, *As It Was in the Beginning* (1934), was her boldest venture into the use of stream of consciousness narrative. The book takes place entirely in the mind of Millicent—Lady Chesborough, widow of Lord Harold—as she lies in a nursing home, dying from the effects of a stroke. Nurses come in and go out, always adjusting her sheets, lifting her numb left arm as they do. As Millicent floats in and out of consciousness, she revisits moments from her life, rerunning these memories as one sometimes gets a bit of a song caught in mind, slowly moving back until birth and death coincide. Millicent struggles for a sense of self, feeling herself 'there, but not in the body: watching it from the outside and feeling responsible for it, without having it firmly in hand. Having to creep back in to pull the strings.' Trevelyan builds a powerful sense of a woman whose life was a constant struggle to define her identity—a struggle she often lost.

Trevelyan's next novel, *War Without a Hero* (1935), is in some ways even more claustrophobic in mood than *As It Was in the Beginning*. Its story is implausible: a sophisticated socialite takes a room with a fisherman's family on a remote Channel isle to ride out the initial storm over her divorce. She takes pity on the family's blind son, marries him to wrest the young man from his domineering mother, and arranges for surgery in London to restore his sight. When the couple return to the island, however, she herself falls into a battle of wills with the mother and loses, transforming slowly into a grey, hopeless scullery maid. As a novel, *War Without a Hero* is an unconvincing failure. As a psychological horror story, however, it's as powerful as a vortex.

In contrast, *Two Thousand Million Man-Power* (1937) takes the lives of its two leading characters—Katherine, a schoolteacher, and Robert, a chemist (as in scientist, not pharmacist)—and sets them against a backdrop of national and international events. Trevelyan adopts John Dos Passos' technique from his *U.S.A.* trilogy and peppers her text with snatches of news of the world, using the headlines almost like the chorus in a Greek tragedy. Though the couple see themselves as superior to their neighbours and co-workers, they are no more in control of their lives than any other pieces of flotsam on the tides of social and economic change. Robert loses his job and one by one their appliances, car and house are repossessed. They find themselves trapped in dismal rooms with nothing to do but scour job notices and write ever-more-desperate letters of application. Trevelyan's depiction of the grim ordeal of unemployment rivals anything in Orwell's *The Road to Wigan Pier*. And she shares Orwell's cynical assessment of capitalism's effects on the individual. 'That was what the machine had done to them,' Robert thinks, 'shown them one another. Each had seen the other as something the machine didn't want.'

Trevelyan's discontent with the status quo is even more apparent in her next work, *Theme with Variations* (1938). 'Samuel Smith was the best part of thirty before anyone told him he was a wage-slave,' the book opens. Trevelyan's theme is entrapment. Her variations are three individuals—a working man, a wife and an ambitious young woman—each trapped in their own cage. The bars may be economic circumstances, class prejudices, social mores, fear, or just bad luck, but they rule out any possibility of escape and freedom as effectively as those made of steel. Perhaps saddest of Trevelyan's three trapped specimens is Evie Robinson, a bright girl held back by her family's mutual enabling society. Evie's younger sister, Maisie, suffers from some unnamed disability—something physical but also somewhat mental—that draws in all the

11

family's energies. Her mother and father look to Evie to take over the burden of caring for Maisie, but Evie has the spunk to plan her escape. And she does, at least at first, training as a secretary, reaching the head of her class, gaining a spot in a local business, cramming for the civil service exam. But the power of her family's dependency ultimately overwhelms her.

William's Wife, published the same year, represents Trevelyan's greatest fictional transformation. She takes us step by step through the metamorphosis of Jane Atkins from an ordinary young woman in service (a good position, more of a lady's companion) to a peculiar figure haunting the streets of London, bag in arm, scavenging for food and firewood. When Jane marries William Chirp, a middle-aged widower and grocer, the little nest-egg she'd earned in service—twenty pounds—becomes William's property. But this small transaction comes to symbolise William's assumption of ownership over all aspects of Jane's life. As the story is seen entirely through Jane's eyes, the reader is slow to recognise her metamorphosis into a suspicious, miserly, and tight-lipped old woman until the process is irreversible. In the end, long after William is dead, his wife is still at the mercy of his small-minded penny-pinching ways. The ability of Oxford-educated Trevelyan to slip inside the mind, culture and language of a woman of a different age and class is a testament to her powers of observation.

Trevelyan's last novel, *Trance by Appointment* (1939), tells a simple and sad story. Jean, the middle daughter of a working-class London family, is a psychic. As she grows, her family comes to recognise this talent and introduces her to Madame Eva, who runs a fortune-telling business from a basement flat in Bayswater. Eva marries an astrologer who sees the commercial possibilities of a 'trance by appointment' business, and from this point forward the story will be familiar to anyone who's read Tolstoy's *Kholstomer*, usually translated as 'Strider: The Story of a Horse': a vital resource used up in a relentless quest for profit, then tossed aside in contempt. Leonora Eyles wrote in the *Times Literary Supplement*, 'Once again Miss Trevelyan gives us an insight into human minds that is quite uncanny, and her Jean, though such an unusual character, is completely convincing.'

Trevelyan might well have continued to write ground-breaking fiction and become recognised as one of the leading novelists of her generation. Unfortunately, on the night of 8 October 1940, a German bomb struck 107 Lansdowne Road and Trevelyan's room of her own was destroyed. Though rescued from its ruins, she was severely injured and died a few months later on 24 February 1941 while being cared for at her parents' home in Bath. Her death certificate listed her as 'Spinster—An Authoress'.

Brad Bigelow

Chapter One

Virginia Hutton was standing, framed in the white dimity curtains of the nursery window, tapping the floor with one foot. Her lips were set in a thin line.

She was thinking. Thought had drawn two parallel grooves between her light eyes. The grooves met and partly erased those fainter, habitual creases which ran horizontally beneath the nondescript hair drooped limply on her temples.

She stood for some time looking out over the November garden, high walled, where indefinite drops of moisture were dripping dismally from bare lilac bushes and a sycamore on to sodden flower-beds. A file of late yellow daisies was staggering along by the wall: an uneven line of heads bobbing at the end of indistinguishable stems with here and there one bending sickly towards the mud.

Virginia turned from the window and poked the fire. Then, leaning against the high fender, she examined the room critically.

'Well arranged,' she thought, surveying the miniature white-enamelled furniture: low table occupying the centre of the room, chair with safety-strap standing beside it, cupboard near the door, with easily reached shelves to teach habits of tidiness, and railed playing-pen in the far corner.

With the exception of her own writing-table fitted into the corner between the fireplace and the window at which she had been standing, all the furniture was white; so much more suitable she thought, for a nursery. It was a pity there was no room in the cottage for her table to stand elsewhere, but perhaps it was as well it should be here. She would be obliged to keep an eye on him all the time for the first few years. Of course, the furniture would have to be changed as he grew, she reflected, but it was better to have a real nursery atmosphere to begin with.

Here was plenty to stimulate the budding imagination. The white screen was brightly painted with fairy-tale scenes; nursery rhymes formed the subject of the deep frieze binding the white walls. Some low book-shelves between the door and fireplace, where they caught the light from the windows, were stocked with gaily backed picture books and annuals.

'No toys,' she mused. 'But that will come later.'

Otherwise nothing could be better, from the blue-ribboned baby basket beside the cot to the carpet of a deeper blue, thick and soft for little knees in their first tumbles. The cot stood under the window farther from the fire, for Virginia was hygienically minded. She glanced across now at the blue-ribboned coverlet and frilly white pillow. The clothes were very slightly mounded and the top of a tiny dark head just showed above the edge of the sheet. There was no movement or sound.

Sitting balanced on the high fender, her fingers tapping its brass edge, Virginia frowned a little anxiously.

'It should do,' she said half aloud. 'If he doesn't turn out well, at least it won't be the fault of early environment.'

She sat silent for a time, contemplating the tiny dark splash in the whiteness of the cot. Then she started and looked at her watch.

'Time for his bottle.'

She hurried out of the room.

Chapter Two

Virginia came briskly into the nursery and shut the door with decision. She crossed the room and glanced out of the window. A heavy fall of snow had covered the lawn, and the nursery was filled with the flat, dead light reflected from it. Only within range of the fire had the whiteness taken on a tinge of yellow.

Virginia consulted the thermometer which hung on the wall between the windows and found that in spite of the weather the room was sufficiently heated. Then, remembering her purpose, she turned towards the cot where the smooth, frilly pillow was uncreased and the blue-ribboned coverlet flat except for a mound just below the pillow as if a tiny body were hunched up there.

Gently Virginia turned back the clothes and uncovered a small dark head with face buried in two tiny crinkled hands.

She stood holding the edge of the sheet. Her lips relaxed into a momentary smile as she very softly stroked the head with the finger-tips of her disengaged hand.

'Appius,' she said.

A little sleepy grunt answered her and the small body burrowed more determinedly. Firmly, though gently, she unclenched the crinkled hands and raised the pink baby face on to the pillow. It was crumpled into a million tiny folds, eyes tightly screwed in sleep.

'Head out,' she said firmly, and turned back sheet and blanket from the rest of Appius. A little furry body, half squirmed out of a long flannel garment, lay with knees drawn tightly up to the chin.

Virginia rearranged the flannel, tucked in the sheet and blanket, gave a light pat to the coverlet and recrossed the room to her writing-table by the fireplace.

Appius went on sleeping.

Miss Hutton opened a book of the kind supplied by infants' food manufacturers and headed 'Appius.' Dating a new page, she made the entry, 'Still sleeping with head covered.' Then she took up a larger notebook and absently fingered the pages.

Here and there an entry caught her eye, and she read: '… to-day Appius was brought to the cottage. As yet he seems to be hardly conscious of his surroundings.'

And earlier: 'To-day found the very cottage, some distance from any house, and well shut in. Small and easy to work, for I think it will be better to have no servants to start with. A garden for exercise, and a room which will be ideal as the nursery.'

Then, some way back, a longer entry: 'Spent this afternoon at the Zoo, intrigued as usual by the humanity of the apes. It suddenly struck me that all experiments made so far in their education have been on entirely wrong lines. I believe that if a young ape were taken at birth and brought up completely in human surroundings, exactly like a child, it would grow up like a child—would, in fact, become a child; except for its appearance, of course, and even there something might be done... If only it were possible to make an exactly right environment and then find an ape young enough to have had no ape education at all, a perfectly blank page to work upon... A dealer might know of one.'

Virginia let the pages flutter loose and sat, with hands folded, looking back through the past weeks.

'I want a newly-born ape. The kind most like man,' she had said.

The dealer had pursed his lips as if he were going to whistle and then scratched his head under his grease-stained hat.

'A young orang, I might get you...'

Fluttered by her daring, half intoxicated by the thrill of the experiment and insensibly by the warm smell of dog, monkey and parrot crammed in close proximity, she had murmured, 'Yes, that would do. You might let me know. Any time within the next week or so...' and gone from there to a house agent's and in a few days to the nursery department of a large store.

So that was the beginning.

After all, what was there to prevent her making this experiment if she chose? Indulging this whim, then? She answered, a little defiantly, the silence of the white and blue room.

She had only to give notice at the club. Nobody was interested in, or indeed noticed, her departure except a few tradespeople. Besides, she had always meant to come back to the country ever since father died and the vicarage had to be given up. But the club was convenient, and there had been no reason to give notice on one day rather than another.

Besides, she'd always had an idea, since she'd come down from Cambridge, that she might try some kind of scientific research; only there'd been the parish. And then when father died she had been down for more than ten years already, and was rather rusty, perhaps… But here, in her own cottage, she had the material for such an experiment as had never been.

Her glance wandered dreamily towards the cot in the corner where Appius lay tightly curled under the clothes.

She got up, her figure taut once more, her indeterminate mouth stiffened. Raising the sheet, she laid her hand lightly but firmly on Appius's minute shoulder.

'Head out,' she said.

An eye unscrewed itself and blinked brightly at her from between two crumpled fingers.

'Head out,' she repeated levelly.

She lifted the flannel bundle which contained Appius and held it rather awkwardly in her arms.

'The first thing is to learn to obey,' she said, stroking his little pink ear.

Then she put him back into the cot with his head on the pillow and tucked in the clothes.

So this was the beginning.

An eye watched her attentively while she arranged the coverlet, then rescrewed itself in sleep. As she returned to her desk the downy head slipped from the smooth mound of the pillow and burrowed between two waiting wrinkled hands.

Chapter Three

Greedy red and yellow tongues were licking the black well of the fireplace. A black face with red mouths was putting out its tongues at something up the tunnel above it: defiant tongues, stuck out to the root. Sure to reach It this time. Failing. Sucked in again. Darting out a bit further. Quick. Got him. No. In again. In and out, in and out, but the Something up the tunnel took no notice. All the tongues out at once now, all straining, stretching, all joining in one. One huge tongue, point out of sight up the tunnel, staying there this time. Not coming back into the mouths any more. Red tongue with the point cut off. Red handkerchief checked by the black grill of the fender.

Appius was alone in the nursery. The fire which Virginia had just lit flickered uncertainly in its iron cage, took heart and then roared up the chimney. From the cot beneath the far window Appius watched it, fascinated and afraid. When it had become a solid red mass he lost interest in it and stared mournfully around the room through the bars of the cot.

Blue. White. White stripes on the blue. In the whiteness of

the wall above him was a square of pale blue, not bright like the floor but pale with little wisps of white. There were four white lines on it, meeting in the middle, and another below, just above the cot.

Appius put up a hand and touched the lower line. His fingers closed over the edge of the window-sill.

Hand could hold white line. Feet too? A foot went up through the fold in his flannel garment. Two. Appius was standing on the sill.

Hand on white line above him. Fingers won't go over it. Why not? Something there; the pale blue stuff. Hard and cold. Try white wisps. Hard too. Can't be held. Funny.

He looked down. Queer. From his position on the sill the blue stuff was only half the size it had been from below, and not square any longer. Dark things had grown over half of it, the lower half. There was a green patch with a brown stripe on each side of it, the stripes getting closer together at the top. Red stripes outside again, with green patches on them. Some of the green was spilled over on to the blue, and there were patches of it at the end of thin brown stripes. Funny mess. And the four white lines that he couldn't hold were crossing the mess and the blue too.

Hold brown stripe down there. Queer. Or red stripe. Funny. All felt the same. No edge. Not like the white stripes against the blue floor which one saw from the cot and could hold. Cold, too, all this mess, and slippery. Fingers slid on it.

Disposing of window and garden with a grunt of disgust, Appius slid back on to the cot and ran on all-fours around the counterpane, the flannel flying after him.

A white thing he was running on. Blue stripe around the edge with little white things across it at intervals. Could hold that. And pull. Blue stripe came away, and some of the white things came too. Nice noise. Swishing noise with little squeaks in it.

Blue thing all come now. Twisting around his feet. Thinks it will hold him. Long thing, smooth like the funny things above the white ledge, but not cold. And soft. Kill it. Throw it over the edge of the cot. Partly over. Hanging. Limp. Dead.

Another blue thing round the edge of the pillow. Kill that too. His fingers had just clutched the ribbon when the door opened softly. Virginia tiptoed in, her eyes, filled with maternal anxiety, falling first on the cot. She stopped, her hand still on the doorknob, and shifted her weight on to her backward foot, her eyes half afraid. One second, then the hand on the door-knob stiffened. Her face and figure became rigid. She shut the door softly but very firmly behind her and walked to the cot. She stood looking down at Appius, saying nothing.

The opening of the door had cut into the first luscious swish of the satin ribbon. Appius stood arrested in the very act of tugging, his eyes, with impudence glittering through their habitual pessimism, turned brightly upon Virginia. As she came further into the room he wrenched his nails out of the ribbon, squirmed under the bedclothes and lay still. One eye twinkled at Virginia from between his fingers, over the edge of the sheet. He waited. Virginia waited. Then: 'Appius,' she said.

The eye twinkled.

'Appius.'

One bound. Coverlet, blanket, sheet flew helter-skelter and collapsed on the carpet. The pillow, heaved as far as the topmost cot-rail, clung there a moment and then fell back, pulled by its own weight. By the time it had plopped onto the empty cot Appius was scuttling on all-fours round and round the room, his front legs firmly encased in frilled cambric sleeves, and a tattered flannel banner, still attached to his middle, swaying defiantly behind him.

As he passed the gaily furnished bookcase one crinkled hand shot up and clutched the second shelf. Feet followed. Next shelf. Feet entangled in flannel and cambric missed their hold. Appius fumbled wildly, fell with a bump on to the carpet and rolled in a puzzled, jibbering ball of fur and flannel. He kicked, clawed, kicked his feet free and scampered on faster and faster around the edge of the carpet, chattering angrily. Virginia stood still by the cot and watched him.

Growing tired, he halted by the fender and sat with his back to the room, holding out his hands to the blaze and chattering affably. Now and then he threw a glance over his shoulder at Virginia, who was grimly arranging the cot and seemed to be taking no notice of him.

When the cot was made Virginia came into the middle of the room and stood looking at Appius's back. She looked at it so intently that Appius, throwing a malicious twinkle over his shoulder, found his glance suddenly caught and held. He turned half round, jibbering fiercely.

Virginia stood still.

He turned round still further, pivoting right round until he sat facing her, gesticulating. An apologetic note slid into his chatter.

Virginia went on looking at him, saying nothing. His gesticulations became deprecating, shy. He chattered less loudly. He edged backwards towards the fender. His head shifted uneasily to and fro. He was trying to free his eyes from Virginia's, but she held his glance steadily. His chattering died down and began again irritably. He whimpered quietly, raising his hands to his eyes.

'Bed,' said Virginia sternly, pointing to the cot.

At the sound of her voice Appius stopped whimpering. His fascinated eyes did not leave her face but, while still enchained, he saw or sensed the intention of the pointing finger. His whimpering broke out again on a higher note; he cowered against the fender. The crinkled corners of his mouth drooped and large tears formed at the edges of his eyes.

'Bed, Appius.'

The pointing finger did not move. Virginia spoke in the same level voice. Watching her fixedly, still crying, Appius crept from the hearthrug, sidled around Virginia, turning on his own axis as he passed her as if she were the centre of an invisible circle whose circumference he were forced to trace, and crept into the cot. He crawled under the clothes and lay buried.

Virginia laid her hand lightly on the humped coverlet. 'Head out,' she commanded.

The hump wobbled and half an inch of head appeared. Virginia gently raised the whole on to the pillow and turned away. Appius lay quietly as she had put him, already asleep.

Virginia went to her desk and opened the record book. 'To-day Appius seems to have learnt obedience,' she wrote. Then she leant back in her chair and pressed her finger-tips against her eyelids. She was tired, worn out by the strain of conquest. Yet if Appius were really conquered what a step onwards in her plan. If he had learnt to obey it was time to teach him to talk, and if that succeeded the rest should be easy. Why shouldn't it succeed?

It should. All her will power, all her suggestive force, her whole reserve of nervous and mental energy, was not too much to expend on this experiment. For if it succeeded she would indeed have achieved something. She would have created a human being out of purely animal material, have forced evolution to cover in a few years stages which unaided it would have taken aeons to pass, and have proved not only the truth of the evolution theory but the boundless possibilities of environment and early training.

It must succeed. She knew obscurely, inarticulately, that if this experiment failed her existence would no longer be justified in her own sight.

The newly awakened need of her being to create would be frustrated utterly. She would sink back into the nothingness out of which this enthusiasm had raised her. She would go back to Earl's Court and her bed-sitting-room—gas fire and griller, separate meters; to her consumption of novels from the lending library; her bus rides to the confectioner's; her nightly sipping of conversation and coffee in the lounge: to middle-age in a ladies' residential club. Each year a little older, a little stouter or a little thinner, a little less quickly off the bus— 'Come along there, please, come along,' and the struggle with umbrella and parcels through the ranks of inside passengers, and the half compassionate, half contemptuous hand of the conductor, grimy and none too gentle, as she clambers down the swaying steps on to the sliding pavement. Each year a little less bright in the after-dinner conversation; a little less able to remember the novels she has read; a little less able to find a listener; a little less able to live, yet no more ready for death.

She saw herself sinking down the years as in a gently descending lift, but the lift never reached the bottom. The completed descent, the shock of arrival, the jet-starred crown of death, this would be a termination too positive for the life she saw. Nothing so real, so vital as death could end an existence subdued and rounded and worn smooth by the little comforts and habits of her warm nonentity. How should she die who had never been alive? She would slide perpetually onwards and downwards, insensibly gliding upon a soft and gentle slope; onwards and downwards through time, out into a broad, eternal plain.

It would succeed. Appius had now come out of his at first almost continuous sleep and was fully conscious of his surroundings. He was learning to obey her. That meant that his brain was beginning to wake, and it was awakening to an environment entirely human. No ape influence had ever touched him. His brain was a clean sheet for her writing; it was now ready for her to begin her work. He could make sounds. He must be taught to speak before his heredity had had time to assert itself. That chatter just now, she told herself, was not ape language. That would be impossible, since he had never heard an ape speak. It was the equivalent of those meaningless sounds which all children make before they learn to talk.

It was time to begin now. Appius was waking. She went over to the cot and stood at its foot fully facing him, her forearms crossed on the top bar.

She called him. Appius opened both eyes and said something unintelligible. She fixed him with her glance and pronounced very clearly and slowly, 'Mama.'

Appius said something more.

'Mama,' she repeated steadily.

For hour after hour, her eyes fixed upon Appius, she worked at the one sound, leaving him only when it was necessary to fetch his bottle or make up the fire. When, presently, he fell asleep, she waited, poring over her notes, ready to drop the word into the moment of waking, in which his mind should be more receptive. Towards evening, as she repeated the syllables slowly, firmly, tirelessly, Appius's eyes, fixed upon her face, grew puzzled. His wrinkled brow became more wrinkled.

He looked at her eyes and her mouth. He was silent. He wriggled restively. At last he opened his mouth and twisted it, struggling.

'Ah-ah,' said Appius.

Virginia glowed with delight, but she would not yet relinquish the consonant. 'Mama, mama,' she encouraged.

'Ah-ah,' repeated Appius.

Virginia lifted him out of the cot and rocked him gently in her arms, balancing from one foot to the other. 'Mama. Say mama, then.'

Appius's upturned face, puzzled and wrinkled, stared at her as she swayed to and fro. His wide mobile lips twisted like rubber and his throat worked noiselessly. 'Um-ah,' he said.

Virginia laughed softly, happily to herself.

'Mama, mama. Say mama,' she cooed, burying her face in the soft fur behind his ear. She hugged him gently, tucked him into the cot and sprang to make the epoch-marking entry.

It could not fail.

Chapter Four

Virginia was giving Appius his bath. The folding white rubber tub was open by the nursery fire, and Virginia with sleeves rolled up sat in a low chair beside it with Appius on her waterproof-aproned knees. She tested the heat of the water with her elbow and lowered Appius into the bath.

Appius squeaked and wriggled, but Virginia held him firmly with one hand whilst soaping and sponging with the other. He cried, big cold tears rolling over his flat wrinkled nose into the warm water, but she was inexorable. With mouth tightly set, its corners twitching with concentration, she sponged and soaped, then lifted Appius out on to her lap and dabbed his face with a soft towel.

He knew the ritual, knew that struggling had never freed him from that firm though soapy grip; nevertheless, he made as usual strenuous efforts to break loose and shake the water-drops from his fur. When Virginia had held him for a time he subsided; he was tired after the long, nightly struggle. He lay still, staring at Virginia while she dried and combed him, her lips silently working in time with her hands.

As he looked at her an idea seemed to strike him. He was remembering something, something to do with the movement of her mouth and that tense expression.

'Ma-ma,' he said at last.

Virginia started. A warm, tingling sensation slid down her spine and up the back of her neck. He had spoken of his own accord, and his first word had been for her. Dropping the comb she was holding, she suddenly gathered Appius into her arms and kissed him repeatedly: the furry head; the furry little body; the tiny, smooth nose; the wrinkled, mobile lips.

'Mama,' she purred. 'The darling! Mama's own darling boy!'

She released him, leaned back in her chair and smiled proudly at him. Here was reward indeed for weeks of effort. She seized him again, stroked his limbs, kissed them, nuzzling into the silky fur still warm from the bath.

'Ma-ma, ma-ma,' said Appius, brow wrinkled.

Virginia glowed, and reached for the talcum powder.

Be practical. Now he had begun to speak no time must be lost in vague sentiment. All the same it was very sweet, this success; this gradual emergence out of the dumb, animal body of a living intelligence, a spirit which could recognise and name her, which in time would communicate with hers. What would it not teach her? What unsounded depths of knowledge slept in that voiceless soul? What unimagined stores of jungle wisdom, piled up, grain on grain, through inconceivable ages by the experience of his race in dark, undreamed-of places of the earth? Here was a soul entirely incalculable because formed by a world of experiences and sensations unknown to man; a mentality not only of another race but of another species, closed for ever to human consciousness unless some member of the species could become articulate; an entirely new world, new as the life of a different planet, and the key

31

lay here under her hand.

Steady, she told herself. He is two and a half, and it has taken him until now to speak at all. Don't expect too much. Be content with what you have.

All the same, she answered, he *has* spoken, and he's only two and a half. With the time he has before him he may do anything, become anything. But first of all he must become a man.

Yes, Appius must become human before he could communicate with men. He would not lose his racial wisdom in so doing, for since education could not, entirely, eradicate this in man, why should it in an animal, to whom the past was infinitely closer?

So she reasoned, rubbing the white talcum power well into the grey skin under the fur.

Retaining his universal, jungle consciousness he must assimilate man's particular additions to it. For what, after all, was the human mind but an accumulation of successive layers of experience like a section of the earth's crust, experience won by man at different stages of development since the beginning of time? Upon the wisdom of the amoeba the wisdom of the fish; upon the wisdom of the fish the wisdom of the reptile; upon the wisdom of the reptile the wisdom of the mammoth. Such, she thought, was the wisdom of man.

So, too, was composed the universal consciousness; piled up and pressed down, stratum upon stratum, through cycles of evolutionary life, with man at the top, so busy being sifted and shifted into place on the heap that he forgot to look over the edge at the strata beneath him. Only very rarely, when the pile shuddered through some cataclysmal shock and was cleft from top to bottom, was man forced to peer downwards into the chasm and to recognise for an infinitesimal fraction of time, through the gap in his mind's surface, the ape or the serpent or the amoeba within him.

Virginia fastened the last buttons of Appius's cambric nightgown and set him on his feet.

He was one stratum lower than man, she reflected, in the evolutionary rock; one stratum nearer man's forgotten experiences. When he became man he would act as intermediary; give back to man what he had lost; be Superman because Subman.

He had been standing now for a moment as she had taught him, on his hind legs, hands at his sides, but almost in the moment she noticed him he dropped back on to all-fours. As she raised him with a sharp tap on the shoulder an idea struck her.

Should she teach him to pray?

She wondered. At his age he should be saying his prayers as a matter of course. At the same time a conventional creed must not be allowed to interfere with his freedom of thought later in life. He would need to be concerned more with science than with religion.

She thought quickly: Every child says prayers, so must he. Very few are hampered in after-life by what they have been taught.

'Kneel,' she said. Sitting again on the low chair, she pulled him on to his knees, arranged the nightgown around his feet and, folding his hands, rested them on her lap. A pink puzzled face searched hers.

It is time you learnt to pray, little Appius,' she said; for if he didn't understand all she said at first he must learn gradually, as other children did, through hearing grown-ups talk, and not have everything made too easy for him. 'You must learn to pray to God. Now God is your kind father who lives in heaven and gives you your clothes and your nice nursery and all your nice toys. You must thank him for all these things and ask him to make you a good boy. I'm going to teach you a little prayer. When you're older you'll say what you like, but now say this after me: "Please God…"'

'Ma-ma,' said Appius.

Virginia frowned. 'No, darling, you are not talking to me now, but to your Father in heaven. Now listen carefully and try to say this after me: "Please God…"'

Appius wrinkled his brow. He stared at her hard and spoke earnestly: 'Ma-ma.'

He was tired of kneeling, and wanted to jump down on to all-fours, but Virginia was holding the nightdress frills tightly and bringing them back to her knee each time he wriggled them away. She had fixed him hard with her eyes.

'Listen to me,' she said sharply. But one must not show anger with children, she remembered. She forced herself to patience. 'Please God, please God, please God…' She repeated it many times, while Appius, wriggling, listened with his head on one side. 'Now say "Please God".' When she had stopped speaking Appius twisted his mouth and gurgled in several keys. His hands were held, but he managed to slip his feet further and further out behind him until he was almost hanging by his sleeve frills. Virginia jerked them so that he was obliged to scramble back into his kneeling position. He stared at her and gurgled again. He comprehended mistily that he must make sounds like hers, that if he could make them she would let him get up, away from the floor which was hurting his knees and from those pinpoint eyes which were sticking into his. He twisted his big mouth, but it refused to make the sounds. His eyes appealed mournfully to the eyes which held them, but Virginia mistook his discomfort for concentration.

34

She repeated the phrase again and again, holding his glance unflinchingly. She must help him, she told herself.

Compelled by her look, he struggled. 'Ee-or,' he said at last.

Virginia smiled. 'That's right. That's a good boy. You needn't say any more now. I'll finish it for you to-night, and when you're older you'll say it all by yourself. Now close your eyes.'

With her finger she lowered his lids. Instantly they opened again, but she thought it wiser not to insist too much at first. He must be tired after the lesson.

'Please God, make me a good boy, amen,' she said. And then brightly, 'Now, darling, jump into bed.' Appius, suddenly finding himself released from his cramped position, cleared the floor in one bound and leapt on to the cot. Virginia's stern glance followed him, and he lay down quietly under the clothes with his head on the pillow.

He really seems to understand a little now, Virginia thought. She kissed him lightly on the top of his head and turned out the light.

When the door had shut behind her Appius turned uneasily for some time. He could not find a comfortable position. The long effort of kneeling had made his knees stiff. Climbing over the edge of the sheet, he stretched the whole of himself luxuriously on the counterpane. Then he noticed that something had happened. There was no room around the cot; only blackness everywhere, with a tiny dull red patch far in front of him, and two greyish white patches above at his side. Where was the blue floor? And where were the white bars which ought to be all around him?

He drew back with a snarling whimper, back towards the hole he had come out of. But as he crouched in his nest between the pillow and sheet he saw that the room was returning. Very slowly the bars around him were coming back out of the darkness, only they were grey, not white. Still, they were there, and so were the big white things around the edge of the blue patch which was the carpet; but they were all grey, and the patch was black.

Appius put out a hand and gingerly felt the grey bars. Yes, they were solid though not white. He jumped on to the top of them and down on to the floor.

The red thing, what was it? It was on the other side of the black bars, in its cage. The same red thing that used to be big and greedy and make a noise. But it was very small now and almost dead.

He hissed derisively at the sinking fire and climbed on to Virginia's desk and thence on to the window-sill above it. Turning his back on the room, he found that he was standing up against a square of whiteness, very cold and smooth. Very white. Dull white. As high as himself, as he stood there fingering the pane, and splashing over on to a dark patch above him which had tiny yellow dots on it. Very cold.

Appius shivered. He was turning to jump down when a bright white thing suddenly struck the edge of the dull white at one side and grew quickly: a bright streak crawling across the dull patch, shiny, with millions of tiny bits of brightness jumping up from its surface. On the side the brightness had come from, a round yellow ball had appeared in the yellow-speckled darkness, low down, just above the white.

Appius clutched at the golden ball, but it was slippery and had no edge. His hand slid helplessly down the pane, his finger-tips tingling with cold. He chattered. The yellow ball bothered him. Sniffing uneasily, he jumped down on to the floor. From there he could no longer see the lawn, with moonlight glinting on its snow; but the moon itself still hung, alone and splendid, in the window above him.

Appius sniffed and whined. He turned around nervously several times as if seeking something he had forgotten the look of. Presently he sat down with his head in his hands, hiding from the yellow ball, and thought. But his thoughts had no words.

Blackness. Big moving things. Big still things. Big black things. Stillness, whiteness, dazzle.

White lights shooting: bright blades cleaving the black branches. Big silent things swaying and shivering. Big moving things rotating: bending, sinking, swaying, crouching under the light.

Dazzle, giddiness. Blackness, brightness. Round and round, down and down. Bigness round, brightness down. Crackling, moaning. Downwards, roundwards. Round and down. Roundwards, downwards.

Appius shivered, shook himself, sniffed, ran quickly on all-fours around the carpet.

He came back to the window. The yellow ball was still there. Yellow bigness. White bigness.

He shivered and whimpered and scuttled back to the cot. He turned round and round until he had made a nest in the shelter of the pillow and then curled up in it and slept, his hands over his eyes to shut out the creeping, yellow light. For he was a very little ape and the bignesses were very big.

Chapter Five

'Spoon, not fingers, darling.'

Virginia wiped Appius's hand with a napkin, closed his fingers over the handle of the spoon and guided them from the bowl of bread and milk to his mouth. After some degree of perseverance she persuaded him to make the gesture himself and went back to her seat.

They were having breakfast in the dining-room, Appius in his high chair with tray attached facing Virginia across the round, polished table. A glass bowl of pink roses stood in the centre between them; a low bowl with roses cut short so that Virginia could superintend Appius's plate. Doyleys of drawn-thread work, silver spoons and cruets, furnished the table and were reflected in its waxed surface. Behind Virginia an open french window gave on to a rustic verandah hung with rambler roses. Out beyond the verandah, rose bushes in bloom and madonna lilies flanked a lawn white with daisies. It was June.

Virginia as she ate watched Appius, not too obviously, whilst he struggled with the spoon, missed his mouth with it and sent the contents over his shoulder. He tried again. The spoon wouldn't come to his mouth. It would turn over backwards and empty itself on to the tray of the chair which overhung his side of the table Dropping the spoon on to the floor, he attacked the bowl with his fingers, lifting out the bread piece by piece and shaking the milk from it in a shower of tiny drops over the carpet. Sometimes a piece dropped from his hand on to the white bib embroidered in red with 'Save some for pussy.' He lowered his mouth with its big drooping underlip and retrieved the bread.

Virginia said nothing. No good to worry him too much to start with. This was one of his first meals downstairs, and he had only lately learnt to feed himself. Since he had grown too old for the bottle she had fed him with a spoon. It had been difficult at first, forcing his jaws apart with one spoon while she made him eat with another; but then he had learnt to hold them apart while she poured spoonful after spoonful into the large slack mouth. When first promoted to feeding himself he had put his head down to the bowl and shovelled the food into his mouth with both hands. Horrible, she remembered. Like an animal… But now he had learnt to use his fingers quite daintily. Presently she would go round and tackle him again with the spoon, but first she would enjoy her breakfast on this sunny summer morning.

She poured herself a second cup of tea and opened the newspaper. As well to keep an eye on happenings in the world outside the cottage, though for more than three years she had scarcely been further than the front gate. Appius was a constant occupation; he was a career. He was beginning to be company, too; for although he could not, as yet, frame sentences, he could speak, in a way; would repeat after her the names of objects she pointed out, so long as he could watch her face as she spoke. Was it possible, she wondered, that he was learning by some process of lip-reading?

Carelessly she turned the pages of the paper. There was no news, of course. What news could assert its importance in face of the object of engrossing interest which she had always before her?

She glanced across the table. Appius had finished the bread and was drinking the milk which remained, tipping the bowl with both hands until it almost disappeared into his mouth, and gulping thirstily.

Naturally there were no letters. The postman scarcely ever called at the cottage nowadays except to deliver the monthly bills. When she had first come here with Appius there had been a stream of correspondence for a week or so, forwarded from her London club. Rumours of her experiment had got abroad, and people she had not heard from for years, college friends and parishioners of her father's, had developed a sudden interest in her whereabouts. Dear Virginia, so long since I've heard from you. What are you doing now, I wonder? Are you still living in London, or have you taken up research?...

She had imagined them, as she tore up the sheets, discussing her.

Old students, meeting in Cambridge: Have you heard about Virginia Hutton? Gone right off her bat. Living with an ape somewhere in the country... No, an ape; how absurd you are. Trying to develop its human characteristics...

And parish workers, going into unofficial committee over the teapot: Have you heard? Poor Virginia. They say she's gone quite mad. Doing some terrible experiments with animals; trying to make them human. And disappeared from London; no one knows where she's living. Poor Mr. Hutton, what a mercy he's gone. So very distressing. I always said Virginia was terribly unbalanced…

Unbalanced. That's what they'd all say; what they'd always said: all of them sniggering when she wasn't looking. Ever since she'd left school, and even there…

Well, she hadn't answered their letters, their prying, impudent letters… Pretending to be friendly; trying to tear away from her the sheltering veil of her privacy, to trample with their sneering curiosity on this home she had built up with hard toil and hard thought; trying to break her happiness.

For she was happy. She felt younger, too, and looked it, in spite of the hard work she had done these last three years: for she had been afraid to have a servant; afraid of introducing a third person, especially an uneducated, gaping, gross-minded person, into the scene of her experiment where the atmosphere was delicate as egg-shell and might as easily be shattered.

And then there had been the hard mental work, the intense, ceaseless concentration upon Appius and his needs, the untiring watchfulness over his smallest action. It had taken a constant straining of the nerves to detect the first, faint stirring of his brain, the first dim, almost undetectable movement of his thought processes. Yet she was not tired. The constant excitement, the unrelaxed tension, the unwavering hope, intermittently fed by minute signs, that before long he would communicate with and understand her, these not only sustained her through each day; she flourished upon them. Her face had lost its pinched appearance and grown fatter. The lines of her mouth were no longer tightly drawn but attained an expression of firmness with less effort. Her pale eyes seemed less pale. As she sat there in her frock of lilac-coloured voile with the summer garden behind her, cracking her egg and smiling at Appius over the bowl of roses, she might have been a young wife, a proud mother.

41

When Appius had finished his milk Virginia wiped his mouth, untied his bib and lifted him out of the high chair. Already he was getting a little heavy for her, a little tall for the chair. Soon he would have to sit at table like a grown-up.

Taking him by the hand so that he was obliged to stand upright, stooping only slightly, she walked him through the french window on to the verandah.

This was not his first visit to the garden. For a year past, when the weather had been fine, he had played on the daisy-covered lawn while Virginia watched him from a deck-chair or pottered about with a trowel and watering-pot among the rose bushes. By now the square of green with brown borders which long ago had puzzled him from the nursery window had a definite significance for him. He could roll on the grass, which was soft, and, when Virginia was not looking, run round and round it on all-fours chasing butterflies or sunbeams, or round and round on the brown path, which was hard.

On the grass he had been taught to walk upright, and could cross the lawn now, when he was in a good mood, without falling on to his hands. Here, too, Virginia had made strenuous efforts to make him walk on the soles of his feet, although they still had a tendency to turn on their outside edges when he was in a hurry. Less often than they did, though, Virginia thought.

On the lawn, as a rule, he was expected to play with the toys Virginia had ordered from London: a wooden horse on wheels, with a string to pull it by, covered with brown and nasty-tasting paint; a tin dog on wheels; several rag dolls and a rag picture-book full of cows and pigs and hens; a box of large brightly coloured bricks each with a letter of the alphabet painted on it.

Virginia was disappointed that he did not seem to care

for the toys. He preferred nosing around the lawn, uprooting daisies and plantains, feverishly digging up the ground around the little hillocks thrown up by ants, or chasing birds on the lookout for worms. When she tried to interest him in the toys he would play with them fitfully for a few minutes at a time, and unsatisfactorily at that, and then wander off again.

He refused to drag the wooden horse, although Virginia put the string in his hand and pulled with him. He tossed it into the air to see it fall, and the tin dog to hear the rattle of its wheels. He threw the rag dolls about, too; but as they made no noise he clawed away the face of one and left them in disgust, to grab at a butterfly and chase ineffectually after a distant sparrow. Still, Virginia had thought with a tiny sigh as she picked up the damaged doll, it was good for him to run about during the fine weather. When the winter came he would play with the toys in the nursery.

To-day she did not send him to play on the lawn but kept him with her while she made her daily tour of the flower-beds, perhaps because she liked the reassuring companionship of his hand clutched in hers. She strolled along by the borders, stopping here and there to pick off a faded rose or re-tie the bass of a lily which was breaking free from its stake. She liked an ordered garden, a garden which looked well-cared-for, which from the moment she stepped out on to the lawn would give her evidence of her attention and assure her of a beauty she had created.

Appius ambled clumsily along at her side, straining now and then at her hand when he saw something to be chased, but responding immediately to her restraining tug. The gravel path hurt his feet and he was quickly tired of walking upright, but he was too closely watched by Virginia to rebel. Moreover, his attention was soon engrossed by the trees under which they were passing: drooping, yellow laburnums and tall pear trees white with blossom which lined the garden wall and lifted their heads high above it into the sky.

As Appius looked up into them a tingling, swift as an electric shock, shot along his arms and legs; his fingers and toes tickled. The whole of him was gripped by a relentless urge upwards, an irresistible need to spring, to swing, to feel the rush of air past his body as it swung, light and agile, clumsy no longer, from branch to branch. He ached for the rhythmical, pendulum movement which he had never experienced; for the luxury of muscles fully stretched, the ecstatic freedom of every sinew.

Need and response were one. By one hand he was swinging from a laburnum bough which overhung the path, its cool blossoms brushing his face and legs as they swept past; the other groped for the lowest branch of a tall pear tree.

'Appius.'

Virginia called sternly, angrily. She had never allowed herself to lose her temper with him; he had always obeyed her voice or her glance. But what was she to do now? He seemed not to hear her. Already he was on a higher branch, feeling carefully for the next. Now he was on another tree.

There was nothing to stop him. He must be a little hampered by his sailor suit, but this was loose to allow for his growing. She could catch sight, now and then, through the leaves, of its large white collar. Apart from that, only the disturbance of the branches showed her his progress.

Now he had managed to kick off his shoes. One of them came bumping down a tree trunk a few yards from where she was standing, the other had fallen in a cleft between branch and trunk and was precariously balanced there, tipping backwards and forwards as the tree swayed. Now it had fallen on to the flower-bed.

Virginia retrieved both shoes and, holding them by the laces in one hand, followed the path until she had caught up with Appius.

His socks, of course, must be in tatters by this time; probably his suit too. Soon he would be nothing but a naked little ape playing in the tree-tops. He was reverting to type.

In her horror all the concentrated meals of psychology and science which she had gulped in free moments during the past three and a half years were repeating on her mental palate: inherited instinct, reversion to type, back to nature, discipline and free will, the necessity for inculcating obedience, the call of the wild; they returned and mingled, a nauseating jumble of undigested tastes.

Supposing he came down on the other side of the wall and ran off along the road before she could reach him. Supposing he never came down, but went on swinging from tree to tree as far as the nearest wood, or worse still the nearest village, and were there trapped, or shot, or killed by other animals, or simply starved to death.

How could she possibly get him down? If she fetched a ladder and climbed the tree he was on he would swing to another, and she would only make herself ridiculous. Grown-ups should never make themselves ridiculous to children. It undermined their authority. Besides, by the time she had fetched a ladder she would have lost sight of him. How was it that he wouldn't obey her voice? Could he be deaf?

By this time Appius was halfway round the garden, swaying and leaping in the green, leafy shadow of the branches. Little rays of sunlight were stroking him and playing with him, darting out through chinks between the leaves, flickering around him at a tantalising distance, leaping back the moment he sprang. His arms and legs, swishing gloriously among the branches, were loosening a storm of white pear blossom. Soft and shining, like a sudden fall of snow on a sunny day, the petals showered over the path and over Virginia in her lilac frock as she stood on the edge of the lawn, the shoes in her hand, and peered into the tree-tops, silenced, baffled.

Appius had come to a gap in the row of pear trees where in the previous winter one had been felled by the wind. Its survivor on either side had thrown out branches to cover the gap so that from the lawn this was not apparent, but Appius swinging rhythmically, pendulum-like, from bough to bough among the leaves, all at once found himself clinging to a mere twig in place of the firm stem he had grown to expect. The twig sank perpendicularly under his weight. He was not heavy, but it would not bear him for more than a moment. Obliged to swing and hold again without pausing to look ahead, he grabbed at a branch of the next tree. Again an outside twig. It bent, cracked, and before he could recover his balance to spring he was rolling, clawing the earth of the flower-bed, chattering fiercely, the twig still gripped in one hand.

Virginia was over him in an instant, holding him by the dirty sailor collar, dragging him to his feet.

'Get up,' she commanded in a disgusted voice; for obviously he had not hurt himself, and it would have served him right if he had, little beast, behaving like that after all the trouble she'd taken with him. 'Get up. Look at your clothes, what a mess you're in. Do you want to be a horrid little wild animal, when you've got a beautiful home and a garden to play in? And yet you must go and climb trees like a dirty little monkey in the Zoo. Look at your socks. Put your shoes on and come in to lessons at once. You won't play any more to-day after this.'

She shook him violently, pulled him up and straightened

his suit, pushed him down again and pulled on his shoes, fastening them, face grimly set.

Appius stopped struggling and stared at her with wide-open, tearful eyes. He did not in the least understand what she was saying. It contained words—clothes, trees, socks—which he had been taught to repeat after her when she said them slowly, pointing at the objects. But their connection and even their significance in this outburst altogether escaped him. He knew vaguely that he had been swinging, which was pleasant, and had almost freed himself from these extraneous skins which always clung to him, holding his limbs in uncomfortable positions and pulling at his growing fur. He knew that now he was being shaken, which was not at all pleasant, and that he was no more free. The skins were being fastened on to him again, very tightly, all over, and tugged into place. His face and hands were being rubbed clean with a handkerchief so that there was no more friendly earth and nice-smelling tree-moss left on them. He was not free because of all these things. But, still more, he wasn't free because of the steely, scolding voice that went on and on and would never stop until it was satisfied by his obedience, and because of the hard, flat eyes that looked at him coldly and levelly, following and holding his glance so that he could never get away.

Never again, he knew inarticulately by a dim but certain intuition, would he ever escape those eyes, because for one glorious half-hour he had escaped them and lived his own life, his own swinging, rhythmical life, high up out of their reach among the leaves and sunbeams, and then had been forced to come back.

It was not mama who had forced him. She had not been able to reach him. He had heard the voice, but the eyes had been unable to follow. No. It was his own world which had done this. It had rejected him and would no more be his world. Disgusted by the clothes she had put on him and by his unpractised grip, it had thrown him back at her feet. And now he was all the more firmly chained to her because he had once rebelled. There was no life but hers open to him. The voice and the eyes had won. Now, he knew, he would never escape them even though they must follow him through walls and doors. They would always be watching, accusing. He would never play with the sunbeams again.

Virginia finished arranging his clothes and got on to her feet. Cowed, he followed her, walking flat-footed without protest, his hand within hers, as in silence she went into the house and upstairs to the nursery. She pointed to his desk, a miniature school desk made to his size. He sat down.

'Now,' she said coldly, taking a pointer and indicating the pieces of furniture she named, 'repeat after me: "bed", "table".'

'Bed. Table,' said Appius.

Chapter Six

Appius was staring disconsolately at the garden from the nursery window. It was too wet for him to go out. September drizzle was weighting down the still heavily leafed branches and making the lawn sodden and steamy, Appius's hands were on the lowered top of the upper sash, and he was hanging at the end of his long arms which somehow the sleeves of his jersey suit would always make appear longer because of the gap they left between cuff and hand.

Virginia was not in the room. He kept up a low muttering to himself. He did not now try to catch the trees which seemed to be so close, for he had learnt that there was glass between him and them, and not only glass but the whole length of the garden. He knew that the brown trunks and green, bushy tops were not playthings to grab and throw about as from here they seemed to be, but things bigger than he in which he could hide; live things which had once thrown him down and refused to play or own kinship with him.

He hated them. He had never played with them since the

day they had done that, but kept to the verandah end of the lawn and snarled angrily when by chance he found himself at their feet, led there in chase of bird or insect. He snarled now as he recognised them from the window, and turned from them into the room, dropping on to all-fours as he turned.

He picked himself up, however, much as a child might after a tumble, brushed the knees of his woollen suit as Virginia had taught him and walked, approximately upright, though a little stiffly, towards the fireplace where a fire was burning on account of the weather.

He still bent forwards from the hips as he walked, but his arms no longer dangled awkwardly in front of him, seeming to drag down his shoulders as they swung. Virginia had shown him how to thrust his hands deep into his breeches' pockets; this attitude helped to disguise the length of his arms and was so much more manly, too, she thought.

Appius stood, then, hands in pockets, on the hearthrug and scowled at the fire. A month or so earlier the nursery had become a schoolroom. Desk and chair now held the centre of the room, and a row of lesson books, carefully graduated in standard, had been introduced into the shelves, for Appius had already filled one copybook with creditable pothooks and hangers and soon would learn to read. Toys, however, still occupied much of the room, and Appius kicked viciously at an untidy pile of bricks littering the rug as he stood there deep in thought.

At first he thought for a long time about the fire and how it was warm, and then he thought about the bricks he had just kicked aside. They were square things, all alike, and there were a great many of them, so that if you wanted to get rid of them you had to throw a great many times. That was tiresome. But it was tiresome to have them there. Mama expected him to

50

do things with them, put them one on top of another. Why? If he didn't, she did it herself and told him to knock them down again. Why? But he had to do what mama told him. Not for a moment did he question why. She was mama. The name mama, one of the very few words in his thoughts, was a concept in itself, self-sufficient and self-explanatory. All the questions he asked led to that, and at that stopped, meeting void or opacity.

Mama was coming. He could hear her light quick step on the carpeted passage which led from the nursery past her room, which he had never entered, and the bathroom where she gave him his bath now that he had grown too big for the rubber tub, to the stairs which led down to the dining-room and garden. This was his world. He had no occasion to question its limits or purpose. Its reason for existence, its existence itself, was mama. In the nursery she taught him and put him to bed; in the bathroom she soaped and sponged him; she had shown him how to go downstairs without clambering over the banisters; in the dining-room she fed and in the garden exercised him. Her face, stern or tender, was the last thing he saw at bedtime before she switched off the light, and the first in the morning when she roused him to dress. He was absent from her only in the dark and for brief intervals, as now, when she disappeared to prepare a meal. She formed his entire horizon. His conceptions were limited, excluding not merely the unseen but a great part of the seen, and among them there was no suspicion, no possibility of a suspicion, of a state of existence unsurrounded, unpermeated by mama.

She came in now carrying a tea-tray, and with her foot closed the door behind her. Appius turned round as it snapped to, and sprang to the table which had been pushed back against a wall when the desk was introduced. Jerking his hands from

51

his pockets, he lifted the table and with one swing of his arms placed it in front of the fire.

Virginia smiled at him as she set down the tray.

'That's right, darling. Good boy to fetch the table for mama. Let mama tie his bib and then he shall have tea.' She smiled proudly as well as kindly as she fastened the string.

What a great boy he was getting. Very soon he'd be as tall as she was. And how nicely he behaved, too; jumping to get the table ready for her. Once she'd had to tell him about that every day, but now he did it all by himself. He was growing up, of course, and learning to be considerate.

She patted him on the shoulder and gave him a little push into his chair before she went around the table to her own.

It was a pity he still had to wear a bib, but he did make such a mess with the jam. It wasn't that he threw it about, nowadays. He'd got over that long ago, and spread it on his bread quite neatly with his jam knife, when he didn't forget and dig it up with his nails. But really he didn't do that often, now. It was only that sometimes he forgot to shut his mouth in time, or it came open again when he wasn't thinking about it, and then there would be a catastrophe. Only the other day, when he'd had on his nice new corduroy suit... and the suit had had to go to the cleaners. So he'd taken to the bib again. But of course he'd soon grow out of that. All children did that kind of thing.

She laughed to herself. She really was beginning to forget that he *wasn't* a child. But, in fact, wasn't he? Look at him drinking now. Lifting his cup in one hand more than halfway to his mouth. Why, most children would still be using two hands, and spilling it at that. It was a pity he put the cup so far into his mouth before he emptied it, but he couldn't help that, poor dear his mouth was so big. He *did* seem to be growing to it, though. Really one would hardly know he wasn't an ordinary child; she might well be excused for forgetting it sometimes. Besides, wasn't that the very best thing for him—to forget it so far that he forgot it himself, if he had ever known?

Did he know, she wondered. How could he? He'd seen no other children, had no chance of comparing himself with anyone but her. If he thought about it at all, he must think she was different because she was his mama.

When they had finished tea Virginia pushed back the table whilst Appius wrenched at the strings of his bib. She hadn't yet been able to teach him to fasten and unfasten strings and buttons. Smiling with fond ridicule, she untied the string and wiped his mouth and chin which even now he forgot sometimes.

'Can't he take off his bib, then, a great boy like that?' she chid, and laughed softly.

Appius stared and submitted without an answering laugh. This funny noise she made with her mouth open still escaped him. When the bib was off he crouched on the hearthrug, picked up the scattered bricks one by one and put them down in different places. He must do something with them and he mustn't throw them.

Virginia sat down beside him and began to pile the bricks into two columns. There were twenty-six of them, one for each letter of the alphabet.

Appius watched her, puzzled as ever. Why? She showed him the completed columns. 'There. Now Appius must do the same. Look how nicely mama can do it.' With a sweep of her hand she destroyed the columns, separating them into twenty-six identical blocks littered over the rug. Clearing a space in front of Appius, she placed one brick there, alone, and put a second into his hand. 'Look. That on top of that.'

He built a pile two or three bricks high and knocked it

down again. Wasn't that what she had done?

She persisted.

At last he had made a whole column and she started him on the second. When he swept his hand around to level them she caught it and guided it to complete the pile.

He looked. So that was what it was. Two piles side by side, just the same height. That was what mama has done just now, and knocked it down again. And now *he* had done it.

A tiny rivulet of pride was trickling down from the top of his head, making his spine tingle. For the first time in his life he had a sense of achievement, of self-consciousness. He, Appius, had piled the bricks and made them be columns when they had been nothing but square lumps scattered over the floor. He would do it again. He knocked over the bricks and began to build fresh piles.

Virginia was delighted.

'Splendid, darling. Look how clever Appius is. Three bricks all by himself. Now mama will put one.'

She jumped back. Appius had snarled a quite unmistakable snarl and snatched the brick from her hand just as she was balancing it on the last. His nails had hurt her, but she would take no notice of that, only she made a mental note that they must be kept shorter. But he really mustn't be allowed to get so excited and rough over his games. Now he was throwing the bricks about all over the place. They were thudding against the fender and bouncing back into the room. A nice business it would be collecting them. One had jumped into the coal-box now, and there were others in distant corners. That was a quite unpleasant noise he was making, too.

She called him to order sharply. He mustn't be allowed to relapse into this grunting nonsense. How could she know what he was saying to himself in that absurd language? Besides, it wasn't even a proper language.

'Appius.'

Her tone arrested him with the last brick in his hand. He opened his fingers, and the brick fell on to the rug. But he would not stop talking, though he muttered more quietly to himself and bent forward, hiding his face against the floor.

She seized him by the shoulder and dragged him up.

'Bad boy. Mustn't do that. You must learn to play quietly and not get into tempers. Now leave the bricks alone, and mama will show you pretty pictures.' She reached for the rag picture book which lay near her hand and spread it open in front of him. 'Look at the pretty pictures, now.' She took the book on her knee and bent over it.

Appius scowled and turned away from her. He could see one of the bricks leaning against the edge of the bookcase, balanced where he had thrown it. Muttering, he started to crawl after it, but Virginia, looking up quickly, caught the leg of his knickerbockers, jerked him back and sat him up leaning against her. She held him firmly by the shoulders. He must learn to look at pictures—children learnt more that way than any other—and above all he mustn't be allowed to forget his lessons in obedience. But it must be done with kindness.

'Now look at the little boy picking cherries. You see, he has climbed into the tree and is throwing cherries down into the little girl's pinafore. See how red the cherries are?' With her finger Virginia was tracing the details of the picture as she named them, outlining the probable track of the little boy up the tree trunk and the path of the cherries as they gravitated towards the pinafore; pointing out the little girl's cheeks red as the fruit, her golden curls, and a puppy yelping from behind the tree. Appius was quiet, except that he meekly repeated 'boy,' 'girl,' 'dog' during her pauses after these words.

Luckily, she thought, he seemed to have forgotten the bricks, for a time at least, and to be interested in the picture. If so, it was a step in the right direction. It was tiresome that sometimes he should get so devoted to one toy as to refuse any other, especially, as in this case, one which was so definitely educational.

'You see,' she went on, 'the little boy *drops* the cherries, the little girl *smiles* at him, and the little dog barks at them both.'

'Barks,' repeated Appius; for he had already learnt the names of simple actions, illustrated first by Virginia and then by himself under her direction: always excepting 'laugh,' which she had never been able to explain to him. He seemed not to understand how the noise was made, and his attempts at reproduction ended in a grunt. She doubted whether he had much sense of humour but it was possible that it would develop later.

Now she would take him a bit further: 'The little girl smiles because she is *pleased* to have the cherries.'

Virginia paused, but Appius, though he seemed to be listening attentively enough, made no comment. Glancing sideways at him, surprised at his silence, she found that his eyes were fixed meditatively not upon the book but upon her face.

'You see?' she repeated.

Appius blinked but did not look down. Annoyed, she struck the book with a flat hand so that he started.

'You see?' Her voice was sharper this time.

Obediently Appius seized the page she was holding. He was puzzled. He had made the noises she had told him. What did she want now? This was a flat thing she was holding, soft and limp. Must he make a pile of it? But there was only one of them.

Virginia unclasped his fingers from the page and held them

in one hand whilst with the other she traced the outlines of the picture. Slowly it dawned upon Appius that he must watch her finger this time and not her face, for this offered no hint as to her wishes. Yet she was angry because she wanted him to do something. What was it? Her finger was making marks on the paper. Then this was something to do with the lesson in which she made him draw marks in a book, lines bent at the end, rows and rows of them underneath a row she had drawn herself. Must he do *this* now?

But she was holding his hand. At his first movement she jerked his wrist still further on to her knee, held it so tightly that he couldn't move, and compelled him still to look at her finger. The marks she was making were coloured, not black like his, and they were all different shapes: squiggly coloured marks. And there were not only lines but splashes.

As Virginia drew his head lower over the book, and as his eyes followed her finger until they lost a sense of shapes surrounding the book and then of the edges of the book itself, gradually it occurred to him that there was something there which he hadn't seen at first. Mama's finger was following around the edge of a green patch, and the patch was at the top of a brown stem. 'Tree,' she was saying patiently, with an intense, concentrated patience born of suppressed irritation. 'Tree, tree.'

Appius's mouth fell open in a low growl. The word, which he had cause to remember, had justified the suspicions which had been growing upon him. It *was* a tree, this thing she was pointing at in the middle of the white page. How did it get there? But there it was, very small, but still a tree. And there was somebody in it, too; that thing she was calling 'boy.' But *he* was Boy. Didn't he say every night, 'Pleasegod makemeagood Boy'? Yet this wasn't he. Then why was it called Boy, and why was it up the tree when he, Appius, Boy, had fallen from it? It was small, anyway. He's soon get at it. Soon have it out of the tree.

In a second his left hand, which was in the pocket wedged between him and Virginia, had wrenched itself out and grabbed at the boy in the tree. The book was made of strong linen, guaranteed untearable. Appius's nails caught on the edge of the page and, torn away, made a scraping noise over the picture. There was a jagged furrow through the boy's face, but he was still firm on his branch.

Appius would get him in a moment, though.

His hand shot back. This time it was caught by Virginia, who held him firmly by both wrists while the book slid from her lap and fell in a limp heap face downwards on the floor. Appius's fingers clawed the air furiously but harmlessly. Feverishly his eyes and mouth searched the rug as far as they could reach for the boy who had somehow managed to escape and hide. He must be lying there under the book, he was so small: so small that Appius could have crushed him with one hand, and would in a moment. He must have fallen off the tree, anyway. But where was the tree? That had hidden, too.

He blinked in bewilderment, his lids almost sweeping the floor. He couldn't find the boy, but one of the bricks, he could see, was over there by the coal-box. He'd get it.

But Virginia was jerking him upright again, a little further from the rug and the brick with each pull.

'Sit up. What is the matter with you to-day? You've never been so tiresome. Can't you play properly at anything without being stupid about it? Very well. You shan't play at all. Come and sit at the desk and stay there quietly until I have time to attend to you.' Getting to her feet, she dragged him up, pushed him into his chair and pulled the desk up over his knees. 'Now stay there and don't you move while I take the tea things away.'

She cleared the table in silence, piling cups and saucers on to the tray, grimly collecting the crumbs which Appius had dropped on the carpet.

Perhaps she had been too impatient with him, but she was tired. He had been so annoying this afternoon. Probably having to stay indoors had made him restless, but she dared not risk his catching cold.

She began to fold the cloth. He had dropped jam on it again, of course. Really he was too tiresome. She glanced at him, fidgeting at the desk. His hair, which she kept parted in the middle, had fallen over his face in a shaggy lump, and his jowl was sullen and heavy. How hairy his neck was, too, although she was so careful about shaving it. Really when he was in this mood he might be nothing but a common ape, she thought, viciously slapping the folded cloth on to the tray. She was always slaving to keep him civilised, and yet he could look like this. He seemed to take no trouble at all with himself.

She sighed, twisting back a wisp of hair which was tickling her cheek. How tired she was, and now she'd have to carry the heavy tray down to the kitchen. She might tell him to carry it, but he'd be sure to drop it. She had thought lately that she might have a maid to help her soon, but if he behaved like this no maid would stay there.

Sighing again, she picked up the tray and went out of the room.

For a few moments after she had gone Appius remained sitting at the desk as she had left him, silently blinking and wriggling his cramped knees.

He was stunned, as ever, by her anger, which pressed upon him more heavily through her silence than when she stormed or pushed him. Her words rattled against him like hailstones and as readily fell off, but her silence was electric, threatening him with a deluge sudden and violent. Vast clouds of anger seemed to roll just above his head, always on the point of breaking. They seldom burst, but he never remembered this.

As he sat there, something in the corner by the coal-box suddenly caught his eye. It was a brick, the brick mama had prevented him from rescuing. He would get it now. He glanced at the door. It was shut. Slipping out from between the desk and chair, he sprang after the brick, grabbed it and dropped it on the rug.

There was the other, still balanced against the bookcase. His arm shot out and drew it towards him. For a moment he hesitated with it in his hand, then meditatively he put it down upon the first.

At the sight of the two bricks one upon the other something of his former triumph returned to him. He had done this before, much, much better; better even than mama. He could make lumps and lumps stand one on top of another, in piles, side by side, because he wanted them to. Where had they all gone? Two were beneath the window. They formed the base of the second column. There were one or two under the writing-table and one was right over there under the bed.

He crawled around the room collecting, dropping collecting again. He crouched on the rug, building up the towers, tense with the urgency of his toil.

Both towers were high now. He, Appius, had made them grow high above the floor, not once only, but again. Two tall, straight lines. The chest of his jersey-suit swelled with pride.

But a sudden doubt gripped him. One pile was a little shorter than the other. His mouth fell open with disappointment. Then he brightened. The top brick of the higher column ought to be on the lower. No. They were still uneven. They had only changed places.

He frowned and moved the top brick back again. No good. Muttering, he slid it backwards and forwards until in his haste he overbalanced the piles and the bricks fell with a patter of little bumps around his knees, poking him with their blunt wooden corners. His muttering grew faster and deeper. He swept the fallen bricks to one side and began to build them up again.

Now he was quiet. The piles were growing, square by square. Not only his face but his spine grew taut with concentration. The whole of Appius was absorbed in an effort of balance. He was identified with the rising columns; his existence depended upon their satisfactory completion.

The last brick was balanced. The piles were complete.

No. One was still lower than the other.

Appius stared at them, baffled. He was too much puzzled even to shift the top brick about in an effort to make them level. Leaning on his hands in front of his work, his face more than ordinarily wrinkled in his attempt at comprehension, he looked hard at the space which gaped at the top of the second pile. Slowly something began to move in his brain, sorting and arranging images stored there: the two piles as he had once seen them; the appearance of each separate brick as he had put it in place; the gap he was contemplating at the moment. From this array of images so ordered there suddenly sprang a complete thought, complete not in words but in conception: there must be a brick missing.

Appius's mouth fell open with the impact of this thought upon his consciousness. The sluggish tide which had been set in motion in his brain was gathering impetus, sweeping along with it more and more images: Virginia's hand holding the brick; the movement of her mouth as she spoke; the bricks he had collected from different corners of the room; Virginia's restraining grip upon his wrist; the click of the door as it shut behind her, and the relief of his cramped muscles as he crept from the desk. Again the high towers of bricks which Appius had built, and the gap staring at him, and Virginia's mouth as she pointed at the wooden squares.

'Brick,' he said hesitatingly, and his mouth shut again.

His eyelids fluttered with surprise at the sound he had made. His eyes sent a frightened glitter from their hiding-place among the wrinkles. But the tide of images surging inexorably towards the shore of his consciousness had there met with a boulder fixed and unshakable, his desperate need for the missing square; the imperative want with which he wanted the completed pile, the achievement of himself. And meeting this boulder in their course the images broke upon it, rushing headlong with a roar of surge far up across the boundaries of his mind, demolishing as they went all those fences of indifference and lack of effort and failure of understanding which had so far prevented any intelligent application of Virginia's teaching. For the first time the gaping mouth was contorted into spontaneous human speech. 'Brick,' said Appius. And again, imperatively, 'Appius, brick.'

He paused, astonished at his discovery: the connection between the noise mama had told him to make and the fact that the square was missing and he wanted it. 'Brick' was its name. It was Brick as he was Appius; and Appius must have the brick. If he called it Brick it would come.

'Brick, Brick,' he repeated as he sped on all-fours around the room. 'Brick.'

But it wasn't there. It wasn't under the table, nor under the cot, nor by the bookcase. Brick. But it wasn't in the corner by the coal-box either, nor under the window, nor hidden in the chink between the fender and the rug. Brick. It was stupid. It couldn't hear. It didn't know that Appius himself was calling it.

'Brick,' he shouted angrily, tearing up the rug and flinging it into a corner. The brick towers collapsed with a clatter and their parts were scattered over the carpet. 'Brick. Appius.'

He seized the fender, but it was firmly fastened to the floor. The coal-box wouldn't move either, at first. Grabbing it with both hands, he emptied it, upside down, and threw it clanging against the wall. Lumps clodded on to the floor. Coal-dust, accumulated at the bottom of the scuttle, flowed out and formed a black pond, with a grey aura at its edge shading off into the blue of the carpet. Appius sprang back, rubbing his eyes and spluttering with the dust.

But he was not silenced for long.

'Brick,' he bellowed through the fading cloud.

The dust settled. Among the black coal lumps was one lighter in shade, so merely grey as to appear white in comparison with its neighbours. It was square in shape. Appius hurled himself upon it.

'Brick!' The word was no longer a command. It expressed achievement and satisfaction a challenge to whatever forces had for so long withheld the object of his desire. 'Brick!'

It was in his hand. He turned it over and over, caressing it, dropping it, picking it up.

Brick. It was his. The twenty-five white bricks of the fallen columns lay where he had thrown them, scattered about the floor, powdered with black grit. Contemptuously he kicked one out of his way as he crouched, gloating over his treasure.

'Appius. Brick.'

No longer an appeal, but a self-statement, a proclamation of identity, of sufficiency.

'Brick. Appius.'

Chapter Seven

Virginia set down the tea-tray in the scullery where the luncheon things were already piled in an untidy heap. The bowl of water in which she had washed up after breakfast faced her from the sink; a cold grey liquid with patches of thin, whitish film floating on its surface like scum on a stagnant pond. It should have been emptied at the time, but she had been fagged to-day, and forgetful. She tipped it out and waited while the grey water gurgled down the drain, leaving the film stranded on the sink-bottom, slowly oozing towards the pipe. Then she refilled the basin from a kettle on the gas stove and jerked the dish mop out of its holder.

Cups, spoons. How tired she was.

Plates. Some of the jam resisted the mop. A harder scrub. The plate slid from her hand down the side of the enamelled bowl and eluded capture with the mop. Now she would have to put her hand into the boiling water.

She sighed irritably, fishing with a finger beneath the surface which was already studded with tiny yellow butter bubbles. Her hands used to be so white before she came to the cottage. Now they were red about the knuckles, with a suspicion of black, relic of frequent potato peeling, lingering always about the base of the nails and down the side of the forefinger, resisting soap and water.

They were thin hands, hollow in the palm, with square tips contradicting the length of the fingers; hands in which there was enough practicality to dim idealism, and enough idealism to render ineffectual any practical effort; the hands of a personality in which any positive characteristic would inevitably be cancelled out or debased by another: decisiveness by sentiment and sentiment by decisiveness; until each was reduced to its lowest and most negative form, obstinacy or sentimentality.

She had started on the knives, halting to push with her wrist at a strand of hair which had escaped again and fallen over her eyes. It fell back as she bent again over the bowl, and she had to push it with her hand, leaving a wet streak on her forehead. The steam rising from the greasy, boiling water made her feel sick. She drew back until only the prongs of the fork she was holding reached the water.

She really ought to have somebody for the rough work. But she couldn't possibly let a maid live in the house. So it would mean having a woman in by the day, and that would open up her privacy to the curiosity of the village. She couldn't help the woman's finding out about Appius, and then she would go home with talk about Miss Hutton's tame ape. It was no use pretending Appius didn't look like an ape, especially when he was in a bad mood; his neck was too hairy and his jaw too heavy. Besides, how would he behave with a stranger in the house? Then she'd have all the village around the garden gate, gaping to see the ape, calling out, and doing heaven knew what mischief. No. She supposed she'd have to go on like this, at any rate until he grew older and more civilised—if he ever did.

She had finished the washing-up and was attacking the tray of piled-up china with a cloth. The scullery was small and dark, its one window barred. A few feet away, beyond the grill, a high wall heavily covered with ivy completely shut out earth and sky. The ivy was dripping from the recent rain, and its heavy leaves and black berries gave off a damp, rank smell.

Virginia stared at it, unseeing, while she smeared the plates and clanked them one on another.

Supposing he never did. He might stay always at the point he had reached now; obeying after a struggle, knowing the most elementary rules of civilised behaviour, but unable to converse with her; a totally inadequate companion without power or wish to co-operate in his own development stuck fast at an equal distance from man and ape. If so, what would happen to her? Would she be tied to him for ever, or until he died? How long did an ape live, she wondered: a longer or a shorter time than man? In any case he would live long enough, barring accidents, for her to have lost what few friends remained to her. Not that any did, she reflected, remembering her neglected correspondents. Besides, she couldn't emerge into the world again with such an admission of failure, to be laughed at or pitied by those who remembered her. And she was a great deal older than Appius. She was over forty. Giving him only twenty or thirty years of life, she would be an old woman before he died.

Of course, she might get rid of him. But how? Give him to a menagerie?

Even in her irritation she winced at the idea. How could he be treated as an animal? He was used to civilised life, to a comfortable room, to clothes, to food decently served.

Who knew, too, whether his mind were not already awake, inarticulate though he was? She had taught him human speech, and although he had never, so far, spoken of his own accord, he had the power dormant within him. He understood her commands. He was beginning to write under her direction. No. It was unthinkable that he should be put to sleep on straw and fed on unpalatable food thrown upon the floor. If he were not man, at least he was not entirely ape. Perhaps the Australian aborigine was at the stage of development most nearly approaching his, and who would put the aborigine in a cage? In some ways Appius was the more highly civilised of the two. Besides, if he had advanced so far...

The cup Virginia was holding crashed to the floor. The dried plates heaped on the tray rattled together in a series of little taps. Something heavy, fallen or violently thrown upon the floor overhead, had momentarily shaken the ceiling and walls.

Dropping the cloth and without waiting to sweep up the broken cup, she rushed out of the scullery, up the stairs and along the passage to the nursery. Thrown against the door by her own haste, she leant against it for several moments, her hand on the knob. Her heart was beating loudly from the run upstairs, from anxiety and anger. Anxiety was strongest. Suddenly she flung open the door, her eyes already sweeping the room for Appius.

He was crouching by the fender, playing quietly with his bricks. Then what was that noise?

In a fraction of a breath her glance had fallen upon the overturned scuttle and the hillock of coal in its black lake. At her exclamation Appius turned round. His pink face was quite grey with the coal dust. She rushed at him, panting with anger.

'Come here at once. You'll have your face washed and go straight to bed. No more playing to-day.'

As she reached him, Appius looked up, his face radiant.

'Appius,' he said with intense satisfaction. And then, in a climax of triumph, 'Brick.' Virginia, her mouth opened to scold, was struck dumb on an indrawing of breath. Never before, except to call her, had he spoken without being prompted, and there was, too, something arresting about this emphatic, personal announcement, something which marked it as totally different from his careful imitation of her examples.

'Appius! Oh, good boy! Tell mama some more. What has the naughty brick been doing to Appius?'

She was on her knees beside him on the carpet where the mat ought to have been; but its absence, and the overturned scuttle and even the dust on Appius's face, had faded from her consciousness. He had spoken. He was thinking for himself. Here was the opportunity to teach him more whilst his mind was receptive.

'Look, darling,' she said, picking up one of the discarded bricks and joining it to his grey one. 'Look. Two bricks now.'

'Brick,' said Appius with unaltered satisfaction.

'No. *Bricks*, darling. Look, there are two of them. Now this is brick.' She put one behind her. 'And these are *bricks*.' She withdrew it and placed both in front of him. 'Now be a good boy and say "bricks".'

'Brick,' he said.

'No.' She put one in his hand. 'Brick.' She held up the other. 'Now,' and she made him hold them, 'bricks.'

Appius began to look puzzled.

'Brick,' he said more doubtfully. Then, with an air of sudden comprehension, 'Brick. Appius.'

She laughed. So he hadn't understood her. It was the verb he was looking for. Should she try him with 'holds' or 'has'? 'Holds' perhaps was easier to explain. Removing one of the bricks, she closed his fingers around the other. 'Appius holds brick,' she said, smiling.

Appius frowned.

'Appius. Brick,' he repeated with determination, dropping it.

Virginia braced herself for an effort. The coal-dust which still hung thickly in the air was parching her throat and stinging the back of her nose, but she would persevere.

'Holds,' she repeated, her smile fixed and calm. 'Holds, holds.' She picked up a brick, made him hold it, held it herself. She repeated the verb many times, fixing his attention with her gaze.

Appius watched her silently, then in one of her pauses he spoke. 'Holds,' he said flatly and without conviction.

Virginia clapped her hands.

'Splendid, darling. Now say the whole sentence, "Appius holds bricks".'

'Holds,' he repeated irritably. He was beginning to fidget, his eyes wandering restlessly about the room. He leaned back and grabbed at some of the scattered bricks, dropping them one on another. 'Brick. Appius,' he muttered defiantly.

He's tired, thought Virginia, relenting.

Aloud she said brightly, relaxing the pucker of concentration between her brows, 'All right, darling. We won't bother him any more tonight. He's been a good boy, and to-morrow he shall learn to talk some more, like a big man. Let mama give him his bath and he shall go to bed.'

Getting up, she moved over to the cot and turned down the sheet. He knew the signal, and was on his feet, struggling with his jersey, when she turned round. By the time she had taken his dressing-gown from the cupboard he was involved with the knickers. The braces were too much for him, but he stood quietly while she unfastened them and helped him into the camel's-hair dressing-gown, knotting its red cord. Then he followed her to the bathroom.

How quickly he was growing, she thought as she soaped him. Soon she would have to teach him to wash himself, but it was so difficult to keep him clean; and it would be increasingly difficult as his hair grew longer. Luckily it wasn't very thick; with care the greyish skin could be got at fairly easily through the wide partings. But of course drying him was a terrible business, and it might be fatal for him to go to bed wet. There was just a chance the hair might disappear as he grew older, with wearing clothes all the time. She wondered. It would certainly be more convenient and would look better, too; though it really didn't show except at his neck and wrists.

'Brick,' said Appius contentedly, seizing the soap as she replaced it in the dish.

'Soap, darling,' she admonished him absent-mindedly, busy with the sponge.

'Appius,' he said.

Now to dry him. 'Come along, quick.'

She stood ready with the towel as he clambered over the edge of the bath, shaking himself so that a cloud of drops broke about the room. She rubbed energetically whilst he played with the soap, which he had brought out with him, tossing it from one hand to the other until it fell and slid out of his reach, making a white, slippery track across the checked linoleum.

'Brick,' he called after it commandingly. The soap took no notice.

'Stand still, darling,' Virginia murmured. 'Now for his toes.'

She knelt on the floor, lifting one foot at a time while he wriggled and stretched in the direction of the soap. At last she got him into his pyjamas and dressing-gown and let him go. Immediately he pounced upon the soap and squeezed it in his hands until they were all sticky and white. Then she took it from him.

'Appius,' he said indignantly.

'No, dear. Come along and mama will give him a brick instead, to take to bed with him.' She led him back to the nursery, and seated herself on a chair. 'Prayers first,' she warned.

'Brick,' he insisted fretfully.

She gave in, for it was late, and he knelt at her knee with the brick clasped between his uplifted hands.

'Pleasegod makemeagood boy. Brick,' he ejaculated.

Virginia laughed. Really he was so sweet with his little, clean, pink face coming out of his blue-striped pyjamas that she couldn't scold him this time.

'Now into bed.'

She untied the dressing-gown rope. In a second he was in the cot, the brick still tightly clasped. She tucked him in and stood looking down at him as his eyes shut and his grasp upon the brick relaxed. The affection which all day had been goaded into annoyance flowed back into her as she watched him. How could she have thought about him as she did in the scullery? He was so good, really, so sweet and child-like. All he needed was a little loving understanding. Anger closed him into himself, brought out the animal part of him, but under kindness he expanded. He was just like a child to-night, so trusting and affectionate. She bent and kissed him very gently on the downy back of his head.

He was a child, really. Her child. She would always protect him, try never to fail him by misunderstanding, and as he grew older he would learn to understand and love her.

Tiptoeing across the room, she carefully collected the lumps of coal into the scuttle, leaving the dust to be swept up in the morning; drew back the curtains, switched out the light and left him.

Outside Appius's window the clouds had lifted, and a full moon was rising in a clear sky. Its light flowed over the garden, bleaching the lawn and pear trees, and shone into the nursery full upon the cot.

But Appius did not see it. He was fast asleep with the brick lying quietly beside him where it had slipped from his relaxing hand.

Chapter Eight

'Snow falls. Appius cold.' He shivered, with one hand rubbing the frost from the pane. 'Snow cold. Garden cold. Appius walk fire.'

He turned towards the hearth where there was an enormous blaze, for in this weather Virginia was more than usually anxious about his health.

It had been a long winter, and now, in early March, there was still snow on the ground. Appius had scarcely left the house for several months, but the lack of exercise did not seem to disagree with him. He had grown a good deal. All his clothes had had to be changed and a small bed had replaced the cot. As he stood now, warming his hands at the fire, the top of his head reached more than half-way to the mantelpiece.

'Fire hot,' he murmured appreciatively. 'Appius hands hot.'

Virginia was not in the room. He often spoke to himself now; it helped him to remember what he meant to do, and was useful in impressing his approval or disapproval upon objects around him. 'Fire hot Appius legs,' he commanded. Turning his back to it, he leant against the fender, hands in pockets. While the comfortable warmth crept along his limbs his deep-set eyes wandered carelessly around the room. There was nothing in it to attract his attention; no piece of furniture which he had not either known all his life or recently seen introduced and closely examined. In fact, there was nothing interesting in the room except himself. He glanced down along the length of his grey flannels, from the middle of the chest, which was the first point he could see over his prominent jaw, to the knees where there was just an inch or so of dark hair showing between the end of the knickerbockers and the beginning of the warm, grey woollen socks. Stout shoes firmly planted on the rug almost horizontally to the fender supported him in his leaning position.

'Appius. Big boy,' he noted with satisfaction. 'Big boy, Appius.'

For some time he turned the thought in his mind until the heat penetrating his socks diverted his attention.

'Appius hot. Appius play train.'

Slowly balancing himself upon his feet, he walked across to the cupboard, opened it and took out a clockwork train. Having carried it back to the fire, he crouched upon the floor, the train clutched in his right hand, arms outstretched on either side to the ends of the rug. Pushing the train with the full force of one hand, he drove it towards the other, which caught and sent it back. The train shot backwards and forwards over the rug.

'Appius play train,' he announced to the fire. 'Train run.'

The train was rather battered, its engine funnel crooked and one of its coaches with a side caved right in, whilst all were liberally dented and scratched. These injuries dated from the arrival of the train, when Virginia had wound up the clockwork and set it in motion across the floor. Appius had caught and banged it against the fender until it was dead and couldn't run any more. Why should it run in his nursery? After that Virginia had crossly taken it from him and hidden it at the back of the cupboard; until he should be old enough to appreciate it, she said. When he had found it the other day he had thought it quite a nice thing which would run when he told it to. It couldn't run any more by itself.

'Appius play train,' he explained as the door opened.

'Yes, darling.' Virginia smiled. 'Shall mama make it run for him?'

As he took no notice of her offer she thought it better, remembering previous attempts, not to insist, but hovered behind him while he played, making no comment but remarking the strength of his muscles and the force with which the train was shot from hand to hand. Presently he grew tired of the game, and heading the train away from him, propelled it violently from behind. It collided with the fender and lay fallen on its side. He gave it an impatient push with his foot.

'Appius want,' he muttered sullenly. He was not sure what he wanted, but it was something different.

Virginia pulled up an easy chair to one side of the rug and sat down, drawing Appius towards her.

'Come and read to mama,' she begged, pulling him on to her knee.

'Appius want.'

He was getting fretful now, but he wriggled on to her lap and sat quietly in the angle of her arm, hanging by one hand from her shoulder, while she turned the pages of his reading-book. It had large-type sentences of simple words with a picture at the top of each page to show what the sentence was about.

75

Appius wriggled into a more comfortable position and was silent. It was warm on mama's lap. Usually he sat at the desk to do lessons, but this was not really lesson time. He must learn to read for pleasure, Virginia thought.

Reading bored him, but by now he knew most of the sentences in the book. So long as he could say the right one for each sentence mama was satisfied, he knew, and would go on talking for a long time, hum-hum in the distance, whilst he could nod at the flames or wallow drowsily in the warm, comfortable world deep down inside him. There it was always cuddly and dark, like being wrapped up in his eiderdown, only with little flickers of light playing about in the darkness. All movements, there, were very slow and gentle; just enough to make the stillness more delicious, like stretching downwards in bed, half awake, and finding the cold part of the sheets and then curling back into the soft cuddly warmth.

Mama knew nothing of this world of his. She didn't know the way to get there. He didn't know it himself, except that he had to sink deep down somewhere inside him and that he got there more quickly when he shut his eyes. There were no words there, only pictures sometimes: big things, slow and hazy, not like the pictures in mama's book. He didn't know what the pictures were, either. He never could remember when he came up again into the nursery and found mama talking and looking at him.

What was she saying now? He'd better repeat it, or she'd shake him, and then he'd be jerked right up into the nursery so suddenly that he wouldn't be able to get back again for a long time.

'The cat sat on the mat.' His speech was clear and deliberate, the words toneless and widely separated.

Virginia's thin voice followed his. 'Now show mama the

cat. Cat.'

His finger wavered drowsily above the picture until it stopped at the right point.

'Good boy. Now the mat.'

His finger shifted.

'That's right. Like this, you see. Mat.' She indicated the hearthrug.

'Mat,' he repeated sleepily and rather sulkily. Why did she want to shuffle her feet about like that and make him look at things in the room? That was a different lesson. But she was going on now about the picture.

'There, you see. There's the mat, just like this, and a big cat sitting on it. Presently the cat will catch the rat.'

He had settled back against her shoulder and was sinking, sinking gently into a warm, padded tunnel; softly sinking through dark, padded leaves that swish-swished as they parted in front of him. He thought he would catch one as he sank past, but his eyes were too heavy to hold open and he couldn't see the leaves properly, and somehow his hands were heavy too. But it didn't matter, because now he was falling into something darker and thicker and downier, something that seemed to wrap him all around and close his eyes with warm fingers, while the great padded leaves fanned him ever so gently, swish-swish; softer, more muffled, swosh-swosh…

'Darling! You're not asleep?'

Virginia shook him a little, reproachfully. For some minutes she had been suspicious; his repetitions had been getting more and more drowsy. Still, they were correct. He was learning to read nicely. He could start on words of two syllables next week.

'Come along.' Her voice was brisk but not cross. 'The cow is in the field.'

Abruptly, swiftly, with a rasp of tearing tendrils, Appius was whisked upwards through the tunnel and sat up, blinking, in the lighted nursery.

'Field. Field.' He was clinging desperately on to the last word, which had reached him as he emerged.

'The cow is in the field,' she repeated patiently. 'You've done this before.'

He repeated the sentence after her. He was sitting upright now, his eyes very bright. Unfalteringly he went through the remainder of the book, repeating sentences and indicating objects.

Virginia was pleased. Dropping the book on to the floor beside her and relaxing in her chair, she drew Appius's head back against her shoulder and talked, holding him in her arms.

'Appius clever boy. Appius has read all the book now. Tomorrow he'll start a beautiful new book mama has got for him. Soon he'll be able to read all the books in the shelves there. And soon he'll know more than mama. Just think of that. Appius likes reading. Appius wants to read great big books, doesn't he?'

He was sinking gently, very gently, into the mouth of the tunnel. It was still there, waiting for him, holding out its swishing, luscious fronds. Virginia's voice lulled him from a great distance, like a droning of insects heard dimly through the leaves.

The droning had stopped. He rose momentarily towards the mouth. Tendrils still clasped his feet.

She was asking him something. He grunted drowsily. Perhaps she would be satisfied.

She smiled softly. 'The little rascal. Soon he'll be too clever for mama. He'll be a great big clever man and know everything. All the world will know what a big clever man Appius is, and they'll come and ask him to tell them what they don't know, and teach them, because he's so wise and knows all the secrets of the world. And he'll have forgotten his little foolish mama who taught him to read.'

She talked on dreamily, lulled by the heat of the fire and the warm bundle of Appius packed in her arms. Over his head she peered into the centre of the fire, a glowing cavern, scarlet-roofed, in which the flames were stilled. She saw Appius, ten, twenty years hence, a great man, even a prophet perhaps, holding in his grasp all the knowledge of humanity and combining with it the subtle race-wisdom of his forest ancestors. He could think. He had learnt to read. He would bring to his learning an untired brain and a completely untouched stock of mental energy. His physical strength, too, would be greater than that of an ordinary man, and this, because he had learnt to think, would be transformed into brain power. He had boundless possibilities. He would be tireless. He would be able to do more in ten years than any man had achieved in a lifetime.

She talked on, forgetting that she had long passed the limits of his understanding, not noticing that his eyes were closed.

Perhaps he would lead a world revolution or found a new religion. Perhaps he would grasp the secret of happiness which had eluded saints and sages since the beginning of the world. Then he would restore the Golden Age. No. He would usher in an entirely new era, a Diamond Age, sparkling with universal joy: no age of mere gold, with a dark background of slavery and ignorance to set off a glittering patch of culture. The culture he would introduce would need no foil.

She smiled at her thoughts, and started; the scarlet roof of the fire cavern had fallen in. Small flames, yellow and blue, were pushing their way virulently upwards through a heap of black rubble and the room had grown cold. Virginia shivered and bent towards the poker.

Appius grunted as she moved.

'Why, he's asleep again!' She glanced at him in surprise. 'Bad boy.' She shook him playfully. 'Here's mama telling him all the fine things he's going to do, and he snores like a little pig. Wake up, quick.' She bent over him and poked the fire.

His eyes opened and closed. The leaves were very heavy; they were pressing him down again into the warmth. But mama was making a noise and leaning across him. It was no use. The leaves parted reluctantly and Appius was squeezed through.

Virginia straightened herself and sat Appius upright on her knees.

'Do you hear?' She tickled his neck with a finger. 'You've got to be a great man, and the next thing to do is to go to school. How would Appius like to go to school?'

He blinked, puzzled by the unknown word.

'Appius go school,' she teased.

'Sool. School.' He repeated it dully.

She laughed mockingly.

'School. Lessons. Lots of other boys; nice boys to play with.'

He was still puzzled.

'Appius play with other boys,' she repeated.

He considered, frowning. 'Appius play. Boys play, Appius play.' He thought and then brightened. 'Appius big boy,' he announced. He thought again. 'Appius kill boys.' His face cleared. The problem was solved.

Virginia leant back and laughed peels of laughter, while Appius's brow furrowed again. What *was* that noise?

'No, you little rascal, that wouldn't do at all. Appius would learn with the boys, and play with the boys, and make lots of friends, and grow up into a great big man.' She stood him on his feet and got up, yawning. 'Well, we'll see. He'll have to do a lot of lessons yet before he can go to school. Now come along, it's time for his bath.'

He was still blinking as she bustled him out of the nursery.

Chapter Nine

Virginia was in her room, taking down her hair in front of the mirror. She smiled a little, thinking of Appius, as she removed the pins and dropped them one by one on the dressing-table.

How sweet he had been to-night. He had gone to bed quietly, playing hardly at all, and had looked up at her quite affectionately when she had kissed him good night. He really was fond of her, she knew, although he wasn't demonstrative. Children weren't, though; they were too much occupied with their own thoughts to bother about grown-ups.

What were Appius's thoughts? Those mysterious thoughts he relapsed into when he wasn't playing. What had she thought about when she was a child? She couldn't remember. Well, he'd soon be able to tell her. He had been talking far more, lately, even when he was alone. She had heard him sometimes just before she came into a room, though he had not seemed to be saying anything interesting. But soon he'd be talking to her like a grown-up.

How good he'd been this evening over his reading lesson.

And then he'd snuggled against her so sweetly whilst she had talked to him. It had given her such a comfortable, warm feeling, having him cuddled in her arms like that, for all the world as if she really were his mother! After all, she might well feel that she was. Nobody else had been near him since he was born. Every bit of him, as he was now, she had made.

Of course he had fallen asleep, poor child. She'd talked on and on, quite forgetting that he couldn't follow her in those dreams of hers. Dreams of his future.

She laughed gently to herself in the glass. How like a mother that was, to sit there dreaming of the great things her boy would do, and forget all about his bedtime, quite lost in her thoughts.

How splendid it would be, though, if he really could go to school, and then perhaps to the university—that would depend upon the direction his talents seemed to be taking—and make his mark in the world. She would miss him terribly, but she mustn't be selfish. He had his own life to live, her son.

Appius Hutton. A good name for a writer. A name that would suit any profession, in fact. It would look well on hoardings if he should play or act. Song recital by Appius Hutton.

Perhaps it would be best for a scientist, though. Appius Hutton: a course of lectures on Evolution, on Mind, on Race Memory. A reliable name. Soundness and common sense in the Hutton to inspire the public with confidence. No fanciful nonsense here; all facts fully corroborated by careful research. Yet a touch of imagination, almost of poetry, in the Appius, if he should be an artist: something a little remote and exotic to distinguish him from Charles or Henry or William. And the whole, with its blend of the practical and romantic, well rounded and polished.

Yes. It had been a stroke of genius on her part, that choice of a name for him. She had hit upon it quite by chance, too: a stray echo of something heard years before in Cambridge. Appius and Virginia: the title of an old tale, or a play was it? For some reason it had sprung into her mind when she had been faced with the problem. Perhaps it was the pun which had dredged it out of the stream of memory. Strange, those punning associations made by the mind. She remembered having seen that remarked upon in one of those books of psychology she had been reading lately, trying to keep abreast of modern movements. And then the aptness of the name had pleased her, the conjunction with her own. Appius and Virginia Hutton. That would look well if ever they collaborated.

A distinguished name. Appius Hutton would win school prizes, would be clapped by his fellows. She saw him, in Eton suit and shining collar, bowing over an armful of gilt and crimson tomes while the oak-panelled hall resounded with discreet, kid-gloved applause. She saw herself in the front row, surrounded by secretly envious parents and gratified masters, clapping shyly, blushing a little at this honour paid to her big boy, doing him credit by her clothes, her slight figure, her youthful but not too girlish appearance.

She met her eyes in the mirror. They were shining at her, their pale oyster colour glowing to blue under the light, flattered by the blue ripple-cloth dressing-gown she was wearing. Her hair, fallen over her shoulders, had golden lights in it here and there; her sallow skin had taken on a faint tinge of pink. She could still look young and even attractive, she reflected happily. No need for Appius to be ashamed to introduce her to his friends.

'Hutton's mater's all right,' she could hear them pronounce after the introduction. 'Awfully young and jolly.'

She laughed softly again as she tied the bows of the two plaits which hung over her shoulders.

What a fool she was, she thought half seriously, to dream like this. Yet why not? Appius had made such progress already that there was no reason why he shouldn't be clever when he was older. He was getting good-looking, too. His arms and head were coming more into proportion as he grew. Next year, or perhaps in two years' time, she'd get a tutor to prepare him for school. Then she'd see.

Happily she took off the blue dressing-gown and hung it across a chair. She sat for a few moments in her white, embroidered nightgown on the edge of the bed, blue felt slippers dangling from her toes.

He was sweet, that baby of hers, and one day he would thank her for all she had done for him, for the wonderful unique opportunities she had given him. He would bless her for saving him from a terrible fate, if he ever understood. But perhaps he need never understand. Dear child.

She dropped the slippers on to the floor, squirmed under the clothes and switched out the light.

Chapter Ten

'**M**an is a two-legged animal.'

Appius was reading laboriously but correctly from one of his primers. At the end of this sentence he paused to look up inquiringly at Virginia, who was knitting in a deck-chair beside him.

'Man?' he said. His eyes were puzzled.

They were on the verandah outside the dining-room window, Appius squatting on the floor near Virginia's chair.

It was almost summer again, a sunny day in late April. The pear trees latticed the sky with black branches, but already some of the lower bushes were veiled in a grey-green mist and the soft turf of the lawn was stirring, breathing almost visibly with the activities of its million lives awakening out of sight. Here and there its surface was broken by little spirals of earth; its green was thinly sprinkled with white and yellow; a few birds were hopping shyly on its borders, alert for a drowsy worm and awake to the almost imperceptible swaying of the grass blades as a beetle or some smaller insect scuttled between their stems.

Virginia was only half conscious of this awareness of the garden and the faintly disturbing smell of moist earth in the sun. While she counted the stitches of a sock she was knitting for Appius she was soothed into a state of comfortable obtuseness by the mild warmth of the air and the ease of her position in the deck-chair. She was glad that the weather was fine enough for Appius to work out here. He had made progress in his reading during the past few weeks, but he seemed to have grown dispirited and dull from the long stay indoors. It would do him good to get some fresh air and have the garden to play in again. From her comfortable distance she heard the rise and fall of his voice reading the sentences. She prompted mechanically, scarcely conscious of the sense of what he read.

'Yes, dear,' she said now as he paused. 'Man is a two-legged animal. Go on.'

But Appius was still waiting. 'Man?' he queried again, frowning.

Virginia snapped her four steel needles together with a click and looked down inquiringly.

'What is it, dear? Man? Why, this.' She pointed to the illustration heading the sentence. 'Man has two legs. Dog has four and horse has four. Man has two.' She returned to the sock.

But Appius was not satisfied, she could see. He clambered nearer to her and held the book against her knee.

'Man,' he repeated impatiently. He peered into her face, frowning again.

She sighed and laid down the knitting. Of course, he had never seen a man. How was she to explain it to him? It was really very tiresome, this question's cropping up on such a peaceful morning.

She took up the picture and examined it more closely: man, scantily dressed in a leopard skin, balancing a club, was surrounded by dog, lion, horse and other animals in cowed attitudes. Patiently she swept her finger again over the group.

'Animals. All animals. Now look. Dog four legs, horse four legs.' She counted them. 'Man two legs.' She looked inquiringly at Appius.

His face lit up with understanding.

'Appius two legs.' He indicated them. 'Appius man?' But his brow had puckered again. 'Appius boy.'

Relieved, Virginia seized upon the cue. 'Boy becomes man. Boy is man before he grows big.' She explained: 'Boy small. Man big.'

Appius thought.

'Appius small, Appius boy.' He paused. 'Appius big, Appius man.' He brightened, submitting the conclusion to her: 'Appius man.'

'That's right. Now go on.'

She turned the page for him, sank back into her chair and took up the sock. That explanation would do for the present. She didn't feel equal to a long tussle with his understanding. Besides she had not yet decided whether Appius should or should not learn of his non-human origin. How annoying this question should have come up so soon.

Certainly he shouldn't know yet, she concluded, settling the wool firmly over her finger. He was satisfied with this explanation, and he would soon forget the subject. She would not tell him until he was fully grown; then they would laugh together at the trick they had played on nature.

The rhythmical movement of her hands was lulling her again into security and undisturbed well-being.

Appius went on reading while she corrected and

commented: 'Man lives in houses.' (House, houses.) 'Man digs the earth.' (Digs, with a spade.) 'Man rules the world.' (Rules? Commands, orders. The other animals do what man tells them.)

Appius was still puzzled.

'Man rules the world, owns it. *Has* the world. You understand?' Virginia was getting irritated by these interruptions. 'Appius has book. Man has the world and all the animals and things in it.

Appius nodded. He was deep in thought.

'Man has world. Appius man. Appius has world,' he said.

He was studying the new illustration. Man had lifted the club in a threatening attitude; lion had slunk away in fear, horse was busy drawing a load of logs, while dog fawned upon man's feet. Appius looked up from the book, his eyes twinkling with satisfaction, and surveyed his kingdom.

'Appius has trees, Appius has bird, Appius has lawn, Appius has world.' A gesture of his hand swept up garden and sky. 'Appius man.'

Virginia smiled absently. 'Yes, darling. Go on.'

He went on, pronouncing carefully, pausing after each sentence to grasp its meaning, to translate it into the concrete terms of his vocabulary and reconcile it with previous knowledge. Planted in the foreground of his mind was this newly acquired symbol of his dignity, Appius-man. Each fresh piece of information was brought to this touchstone, tried by it, and accepted or rejected according to its fitness for personal use.

Man-Appius was very big. He owned the world. All other things did as he told them. (Wasn't his cry 'Appius wants,' invariably answered?) He built houses. (Wouldn't the bricks stand together when he told them to?) He lived in them. He worshipped. (Worshipped? Prayed. 'Pleasegod makemeagood boy.' Yes.) He thought. (Thought? Think. Reason.)

He puckered his brow.

'Think. Talk inside your head,' suggested Virginia, looking for an easy way out.

Appius not talk inside head.

He turned the page scornfully. Appius-man, then, did not think. Appius thought, but Appius-man did not know he thought. Appius-man walked, talked, ate with a knife and fork; but above all he had. He possessed everything he could see, everything he wanted. If he said 'come,' it came. Appius man.

Virginia's voice cut through his halting recital. 'That will do for this morning. Now you can go and play, but don't get too dirty.'

Appius dropped the book and ambled off along the path which passed the verandah. The new idea went with him.

There was in existence a marvellous being called Man, something which had only to express a wish to have it fulfilled, only to express a command to have it obeyed; who had authority and power over all other creatures and objects, this in virtue of his superiority in building, eating with knife and fork, walking on two legs, praying and talking.

And this all-powerful, supreme being was he, Appius.

These thoughts, couched in more cryptic language, sped backwards and forwards through Appius's mind as he slouched down the path, hands as usual in pockets. His feet, owing to their turned-out position—a fault which Virginia had not yet been able entirely to correct—churned up the gravel as he walked. Presently a pebble larger than the others leapt the height of his shoe and struck him sharply on the ankle. He stopped, suddenly enraged.

'Appius man,' he shouted. 'Stone go.'

The stone went skeltering down the path, driven by a powerful kick from Appius's toe, and took shelter at last under the overhanging edge of the turf bordering a flower-bed. As Appius watched it his anger changed to satisfaction. He had made the stone recognise his power, shown it that it couldn't strike him, its master, with impunity. He felt that in so doing he had impressed a sense of his authority upon the whole garden.

'Stone go. Appius man.'

The bare rose bushes looked at him with respect; the gravel did not dare rebel again as he continued his walk, feet lifted high, strutting with importance.

Presently, coming up with the stone, he gave it another kick, just to show that he could. The stone was caught against a tuft of grass.

'Stone go,' he shouted, kicking it again.

The stone stood still.

Appius was baffled, he looked at it furiously. Then, glancing over his shoulder to make sure that the garden was not watching him, he bent and, rapidly scratching a hole in the flower-bed, buried the stone and pressed the earth hard down on top of it.

Hands in pockets, he strolled on.

'Appius man. Stone go,' he announced defiantly.

The garden did not contradict him.

A blackbird, disturbed by his shout, had flown from the lawn and was standing on the path some way ahead of him, an eye anxiously cocked. His glance alit on it. Bird. Man have bird. Appius talk, stone go. Appius talk, bird come.

Standing still, he opened his mouth and bellowed:

'Bird come. Appius man.'

At the first sound the blackbird appeared to raise itself upon tiptoe, its head cocked still further to one side. Before the word 'come' had left Appius's mouth, the bird had darted over the wall in a flash of rusty feathers; the first syllable of the word of power was hurled after it like a stone, while the second dwindled away and sank like the smallest pebble at Appius's feet. For the bird was out of sight.

Appius was daunted only for a moment. Even while his mouth was open in consternation and defeat, he realised suddenly why the bird had not obeyed. It was afraid. It knew the power of Appius and feared to come, even at his command. Its flight bore witness to his terrifying power more conclusively than the most prompt obedience.

At this thought Appius swelled out his chest and dug his hands still deeper into his pockets. There was no word in his vocabulary to express fear, yet this proof of his supremacy must be impressed upon the bushes, which might have seen him bury the stone, and those sparrows which were unconcernedly pecking about on the farther side of the lawn. It must be conveyed, even if in misleading terms. He opened his mouth and shouted again.

'Bird go. Appius man.'

The sparrows flew away. Appius, with an air of supreme contentment, continued his walk.

He had turned a corner now and was sauntering along the path parallel with the verandah at the other end of the lawn. He had not gone far when he heard Virginia calling him: 'Appius. Time to come in.'

He hesitated. Then he decided upon the ultimate test. He would refuse to come.

He shouted back, not quite so loudly as before, 'Appius man.'

Virginia took no notice. He could see her rolling up her knitting, putting it into its bag, folding the deck chair. When she had picked it up and turned towards the door she glanced casually over her shoulder to where he was standing, kicking the gravel.

'Come along.'

Her voice was quite unruffled. Evidently she expected him to come, had not considered the possibility of his refusing. She had simply called him and gone in, knowing that he would follow.

He shuffled uneasily and muttered, 'Appius man. Appius play garden.'

But he was shuffling towards the edge of the grass. If she looked out again he would tell her that he meant to stay, that he wasn't going to obey her, because everything, even stones and birds, obeyed *him*. But she didn't look out.

He was walking now, rather more quickly, across the lawn. Perhaps it was getting cold in the garden, he thought. Perhaps he wanted to go in, after all. Why didn't she look out? After all, Appius was man, but mama was mama... But he was Appius-man, and the birds and stones did what he told them.

Throwing out his chest once more, he turned briskly through the door into the hall.

Chapter Eleven

Appius was alone in the dark nursery faintly lit by a dying fire and a rising moon. Mama had left him some minutes earlier, after rubbing her face against his cheek in the absurd way she had. Why did she? he wondered. He had never fathomed the meaning of this gesture, nor discovered what she wanted him to do when she did it. Since she had never told him, he did nothing, and that seemed to satisfy her.

She didn't always do the same thing, either. Sometimes she rubbed his cheek with hers and sometimes with her mouth, as likely as not catching a hair or two and pulling them as she did so. Sometimes it was the top of his head she rubbed, or the side of it, blowing into his ear meanwhile. Sometimes she didn't do anything; and he liked this best, although it was usually when she was angry. Then the light would go click very sharply and suddenly and the door would snap, waking him up into the darkness, instead of closing slowly and reassuringly so that he just went on dozing and fell asleep hardly knowing whether she had gone or not.

To-night the door had not snapped, and yet he was wide awake. He had thought he was sleepy while mama was talking, but now he was alone his eyes were wide open again. They felt as if they had been stuck open with something prickly; the lids simply wouldn't shut.

He lay on his back, staring at the walls and ceiling which were black except now and then when they were lit up all over by a sudden spurt of flame. Pictures on the walls, the top of the cupboard, the electric bulb, all sprang familiarly out of the blackness for a moment and then were thrown back again. Then, as his eyes became accustomed to the darkness and as the moon rose higher outside the window, the ceiling grew light even in the pauses between the flames.

Words were racing round and round inside his head. Man, stone. Come, go. Bird, stone. Bird come, stone go.

They were flying round and round, running a race. That was why he couldn't go to sleep.

The words wouldn't keep still. They were round and rolling like marbles and they knocked against one another as they rolled, and bounced away again, and got mixed up. But they went on rolling round and round. Stone-go, man-go. Go-come, come-go.

Words without any pictures to them. Why wouldn't they stop? They must mean something. Stone-come, man-come, bird-go, man-go. Rattle and bump, on and on. They were getting more and more mixed up every minute. He was quite dazed by their speed. Surely he was falling asleep?

He twitched his eyelids to see whether they were still open. They were. And his eyes were pricking, too, because they wouldn't shut.

He heaved over on to his side, with a little grunt which was almost a sigh. If only they would stop. If only he knew what

95

they wanted.

His turning seemed to have stopped them for a moment. Their race track had been tipped sideways and all the marbles had fallen to the bottom, knocking against one another in a bumpy jumble: come-bird-stone-man-go.

At last he could catch them. In despair he grabbed at one on top of the heap and held it still. He looked at it until a picture grew up in the darkness around it.

Stone. Round and smooth and grey. Hopping and twisting and bouncing over smaller stones along a path into the distance, getting smaller and smaller, while the path narrowed: swerving to one side or the other as it struck this and that and cannoned off it, but always swinging back into the straight, impelled by an immense, irresistible force which had set it in motion.

Man. Appius-man! That was the key. The drab, identical marbles took on colour and shape and fell into place like the parts of a puzzle. Bird, stone, coming, going, each acquired identity, each again lost individual significance in forming part of a whole: the power, the strength, the supremacy of man, man-Appius.

Appius sat up in bed, fully awake. Appius man. That was it. That was why he couldn't sleep. His brain was very clear now and his eyes no longer pricked since the marbles had stopped their meaningless chase around the inside of his head. His eyes were wide open but not staring; normally open as in daylight. He was as self-possessed as if it were morning; more so, for he had newly discovered himself, the self he had found in the garden and lost again when he came into lunch, and had been looking for without knowing it ever since.

Appius man. That was it. He had told the garden but he hadn't told the nursery. He had meant to, but mama had called him into the dining-room and made him eat his cabbage and rice pudding. When he had tried to tell her how important it was, she had only made that wordless noise with her mouth open and told him to eat up and be a good boy. And when he had tried to tell the banisters on the way upstairs she'd been quite cross and hurried him to his desk so that he'd forgotten about it.

Appius man. He must tell the desk that he'd forgotten when he sat at it this afternoon, and tell the cupboard and the bookcase and the fender. And he must hurry up and tell the fire before it was quite dead.

He slipped out of bed and padded across the carpet without stopping to put on his slippers.

The fire had almost gone, but one or two little tongues were feebly licking the cinders at the bottom of the grate. It was dying fast. Pride and joy rose in Appius as he watched its struggles. It was dying, but it should know before it died that he, Appius, was man, that he lived and walked and owned the world.

'Appius man.'

Leaning over the fender, he spat the words into the expiring flames. The flames died and fell down flat among the embers. Now there was only a small red glow between the black lumps. Every moment it grew fainter and the lumps greyer. Appius man.

He moved on to the writing-table clearly outlined against the colourless light of the window. Then, as he came nearer, something in the window itself caught his eye, something that was bright and shining and strong although the fire had died. It was the moon.

It was looking at him, almost round and very yellow, balanced high up in a dark blue space above the garden wall.

The trees were far below. There was nothing near it anywhere. It was ruling, insolently, that great velvety sea and the dark garden underneath.

For a moment Appius lowered his eyes. He whimpered and began to turn away. But something was tightening in his brain. The word-marbles were rolling up, collecting together, building a wall, and he, Appius, was standing behind it, defended, defiant, guarding his kingdom.

He turned back and faced the window squarely, jumped, and swung from the lowered sash above his head. He opened his eyes and looked straight into the eye of the moon.

Something within him, buried deep behind the line of defence, shrank and shuddered. But the line of defence held. As he stared deep into that huge, unblinking eye, he knew instinctively that here he had met his rival. Here was his enemy, the threatener of his kingdom, the last rebel to be subdued. And the words, the images, huddled together as a defence, shouted to him to strike, to assert his power, to overthrow this arrogance.

Was he not man? Had not the fire died at the sound of his voice?

Dropping on to his feet, Appius threw back his head and drew in his breath. Raising himself on tiptoe, he struck his chest a hollow blow with his fist and hurled out the last, the supreme challenge: 'Appius! *Man!*'

The moon took no notice.

Appius fell back on to his heels and shuffled over to the bed. His eyelids were very heavy now, so heavy that he could scarcely hold them up. He reached the bed and fumbled with the clothes, but he couldn't find their opening; so he curled up on top of them in his pyjamas and in a moment had fallen asleep. Virginia found him there when she came to wake him.

Chapter Twelve

How hot it was.

Virginia had brought the deck-chair into the dining-room and was sitting just inside the open french window. It was too hot to be out of doors; even this room, though it struck chill after the sun-baked verandah, was really sweltering with heat. The polished table was dull with sweat, its wax sticky. The roses which Virginia had cut only that morning were already drooping in their glass bowl.

Virginia lay back in the chair with her arms folded. In spite of her thin dress she was too hot to do anything. She sat there and looked out dully under the canvas sunblinds at the grilling lawn. The heat had made her face thinner and her hair lank. It lay flatly across her forehead and irritated her by its damp clinging, but she felt too limp to go upstairs and arrange it.

She should really have been sewing, too; mending the trousers Appius had torn on the rake the other day. In this weather she had given him a holiday from lessons and let him run loose out of doors. He seemed not to feel the heat, in fact he seemed to enjoy it, was livelier than he had been since last summer. Yet one would have thought the sun would be terrible for him with all that hair. She had let him leave off his coat while it was so hot, and play just in little, linen trousers with braces to match. He looked quite sweet in them, she thought, pottering so solemnly about the garden with his rake and spade.

What a surprising enthusiasm for gardening he had developed. Nothing seemed to give him more pleasure. Very strange. It had started the year before and was as strong as ever. Quite suddenly one day in the spring, when he had been watching her plant out seedlings, he had snatched the spade out of her hand and announced gravely, 'Man digs the earth.'

Then he had uprooted the whole row with one or two tremendous heaves, dropped the spade in the middle of the path and strutted off with his hands in his pockets, seeming completely satisfied with himself.

How she had laughed. She had been too much amused even to be angry about the mangled seedlings. She had wondered where he had got that absurd sentence about man digging the earth, until she remembered that he had read something like that to her one day when she hadn't been listening attentively. For weeks afterwards, she remembered, he had been full of phrases about Man doing this and that. His deliberate speech always gave it the dignity of a capital. Funny child. What did he know about man, with a capital letter or otherwise? Even in the heat she managed to smile.

His solemnity had delighted her, and since then she had let him have the spade and rake and the run of the garden. It really didn't matter that he disdainfully refused to mow the lawn, water the parched flower-beds or make the slightest distinction between weed, flower, vegetable and empty soil.

Digging was so good for him, and to her his health and happiness far out-valued the finest horticultural show in the world.

It was hard upon his clothes, though. He was for ever tripping over his tools and coming down on the path, or letting the spade slip and scrape his shoes and socks—until she had let him leave them off and put his bare feet into sandals—or losing his balance and having to be pulled, struggling, out of a rose or gooseberry bush. She really must mend those knickerbockers.

She half rose out of the chair, but the movement made her brow trickle with heat and she sank back again. Appius was only just out of sight along the path; she could hear him hoeing violently against something barky.

She called him: 'Appius darling?'

He dropped the hoe against whatever he had been attacking and came at a run. Even he had a moist face, and it was pinker than usual with the exercise.

'Sewing, darling.' She waved her hand towards the open door. 'In the nursery.'

She heard his sandals flap, flap up the stairs and along the passage overhead, and the sound of several things being overturned. Then he was back at her side, one arm curled around her work-bag which bulged with mending. She took it from him and laid a hand affectionately on his arm.

'Thank you, darling. Good boy. Now run away and play again.' She began to rummage in the bag whilst he padded across the verandah and out into the sunshine.

When he came to the place where he had left the tools he picked up the spade and walked on, trailing it after him down the path. The spade clattered over the gravel and scattered small stones to right and left as he went.

He was happy. The sun beating down on his bare chest, penetrating the loose hair, seemed with the point of its rays to dart energy into his pores. He had lost something of his usual lethargy, the appearance of boredom and indifference which he usually had when playing; something, too, of the grim assertiveness with which he had imposed his mastery upon the garden little more than a year before. In this brilliant sunlight his authority need not so zealously be guarded. The sun was on his side, filling him with vigour whilst it exhausted his weaker subjects. Even the sparrows had ceased to hop and twitter, waiting under cover for the coolness of evening. Fading plants bowed in obeisance to him.

Further, had he not fully subjugated his kingdom with the spade? There was scarcely a foot of ground on which he had not set his mark at one time or another during the past months, if only by a single shovelful of soil lifted and scattered, or dumped in a hillock on the yellowing grass. No further proof of his mastery was needed, but digging had now become a habit. Here was a fine open space. Having waited for the spade to come up with him, he set it perpendicular to the soil and, standing up to it, gave a mighty downward push with his hands which were grasping the handle above the level of his head.

'Man digs the earth,' he muttered as a matter of form.

The spade sank in half-way up the blade, but the soil refused to move. It was caked hard. He jerked out the spade and went further, dragging it along the flower-bed at his side, stopping to pull when it got caught against a plant or bush. He wanted a sheltered piece of ground where the earth was softer, where he could feel the spade sink in right up to the handle and hear the crisp, tearing noise it made as it prised up a clump of matted roots. He liked the chink of hidden stones and the soft plop of damp under-earth on to the crusted surface.

Here was a place, right at the bottom of the garden, under the pear trees and in the shadow of the wall. Carefully he set the spade in position.

'Hoy! Look at the ape!' A shrill shout had cut through the warm stillness of the garden; cut into the first squish of the spade sinking into soft fibrous soil.

'Hoy! Come orn up 'ere! 'Ere's an ape wi' does orn, an 'ees diggin'! Come orn!'

Appius dropped the handle, leaving the spade vibrating in the ground. He glared around him, startled by the sudden noise. He could see nothing.

There was a clatter of boots coming nearer, and scrapings and shufflings, and more shouts:

'Weere is 'ee? Let me see 'im! Weere's the ape?'

Dismayed, not knowing which way to go, Appius took a step towards the wall. As he left the shade of the pear trees a chorus of howls broke out above his head: 'Hoy ! 'Ee's got trowsis orn! An ape wi trowsis orn! Hoy! Look at the ape wi' trowsis orn!'

Appius was glaring from side to side, seeking the noise. He had never heard anything like it before, yet the hair was stiffening along the back of his neck. Wildly he turned. He was muttering to himself.

At a fresh shout from the wall he looked up. Strange animals with pink faces and dark shoulders were gaping at him, mouths open, and the noise was coming from the mouths. Dark arms with pink hands were stretched out, pointing at him. Waving above his head was a pink leg ending in a sock and boot like his own.

The faces gaped and roared: 'Hoy! Look at 'im! Look at the ape, the ape, the ape!'

There was another, smaller clatter below, a scrape, a scramble and a thud. Then a shriller wail from out of sight: "'Elp me up, I wanter see the ape! 'Elp me up, I wanter see the ape! Hoo-oo.' The faces on the wall went on roaring: 'Look at the ape wi' trowsis orn! Look at the ape wi' trowsis orn ! Look at 'im!'

Appius dropped on to his hands. In a moment he had reached the nearest tree-trunk. But after the first swing upwards he dropped back. If he climbed he would only be nearer the pink-faced animals.

He crouched, shivering and muttering, at the foot of the tree. Under hanging brows his eyes glittered backwards and forwards, forwards and backwards, from the wall to the garden, looking for a way of escape. To reach the house he would have to cross the lawn, in the open all the way.

There was nowhere to go. He was at bay against the trunk, and the faces went on chanting: 'Look at the ape, the ape, the ape!'

He had no idea what they were saying, whether they meant anything by this horrible bark. But something in the noise, the gestures, the derisive waving of arms and legs enraged him.

He was crouching against the tree-trunk. Without warning, in a breath, he was at the foot of the wall, his jaw thrust forward, his eyes almost hidden, every tooth bare. He snarled. His arms shot up towards the dangling feet.

The faces yelled and vanished, but only for a moment. There was a scraping bump. Appius had fallen back. The wall was too high for him; it had been raised to prevent his escaping. The top was out of his reach and the bricks were too slippery to hold.

Cautious faces reappeared. Seeing his failure, they sprang up again, bolder than before, arms and legs more impudently waving. Gaping mouths chanted in unison: 'Look at 'im! 'Ee carn't climb wiv is' trowsis orn! The ape carn't climb wiv 'is trowsis orn! Ape, ape, ape, ape, ape!'

In a frenzy Appius tore at the bricks. His snarl rose to a shriek: three high piercing yells. Frenziedly he tore at the mortar. As the yells died away his big throat began to work. The sagging pouch which never before had given sound was working now and rumbling. He threw back his head, and the rumble burst out in a full-throated roar, a bellowing jungle howl.

The cries of 'Ape' ceased abruptly. There was a series of scrapes and thuds on the far side of the wall.

Then Virginia's terrified voice came from the lawn: 'Appius! Where are you, Appius?'

'Come orn!'

Beyond the wall there was a fresh clatter and scraping; there were thuds and shouts and wails, and a scuffle of feet pelting away over a dusty road.

Chapter Thirteen

Virginia was finishing her second darn when she thought she heard a shout from the far end of the garden. She paused between two stitches.

Children playing out in the road. She remembered having heard voices for some time; village voices. She went on darning.

It was tiresome to have the garden bounded by a road; still, it had its advantages. At least they couldn't be overlooked; the wall was too high for that. She had had it raised so that Appius shouldn't get over it when he was younger and bent on climbing. He seemed to have outgrown that now. Good little fellow, quite contented with his spade; not quite six, and as sensible as an ordinary child of ten, at least. It was a shame she couldn't take him to the sea in this hot weather.

What a noise those village children were making. Chasing a cat probably, poor thing.

How he would enjoy digging in the sand. Would he take to the water, though? Hardly any children did, of course, at first. They had to be taught to like it. He'd be adorable with a little red bathing suit and little red bucket. Couldn't she? Perhaps next year, if she could find a really quiet place where people wouldn't stare at him. She wondered vaguely what he would do if people stared at him.

What on earth was that noise?

She stopped working and listened, the hand holding the needle poised in the air, the other, under the darn, dropped on to her knee.

Those children sounded as if they were in the garden. Perhaps she'd better go and look. Where was Appius, by the way? He had gone off with his spade, but she couldn't see him anywhere. She folded her work and got up.

What was that noise now? A scream. It was in the garden. Could Appius have caught a bird or a stray cat and be teasing it? Hardly. He had never hurt anything yet. He seemed naturally kind, nice-minded.

She called him from the edge of the lawn, but surprisingly there was no answer. The garden seemed unnaturally quiet; even the children in the road had stopped shouting for a moment, here they were beginning again, though.

A scream. Another and another. What *was* it? Shrill, stabbing screams. She was frozen for a moment, transfixed by these sounds which were neither human nor animal.

Then she began to run, stumbling across the lawn almost before the thoughts which had prompted the running had reached her consciousness. They jolted in her mind as she ran. Not a bird. Not a cat. Appius? Appius himself? Had he hurt himself? And she called out as she ran: 'Appius!'

But he didn't answer.

Then, as she reached the middle of the lawn, the village voices localised themselves at the wall facing her beyond the trees. A jumble of noises rose again as the screams died down, and now she could distinguish a word: 'Ape, ape, ape,' repeated

107

and taunting.

'Appius,' she screamed, and ran faster, while there flashed through her mind: 'But he won't understand.'

Now a rumbling noise was rising from somewhere, like thunder in the distance, coming nearer. It rolled on; it swelled into a roar and broke, drowning the taunts, submerging the whole garden.

Virginia shrieked against it: 'Appius!' For she knew now with certainty, and knew that she had known all the time, that those animal noises were his. 'Appius, where are you, Appius?' As the roar sank into a rumble and died away she heard the terrified children retreating up the road, and knew that she was alone with him.

She stood still on the lawn. She wondered whether she would go on, or whether she would go back over the grass and across the verandah and through the hall and up the stairs and into her room behind a locked door. She stood with clasped hands and swayed almost physically with indecision.

That was an animal cry, she told herself. He's reverted to type. He's dangerous. He would have attacked those boys if he could, and he may attack you if you go to him.

Nonsense, she answered. They were teasing him. He had never seen them before. He was frightened. He knows me; he wouldn't hurt me.

Liar, she said. He would, and you know it. Go back to the house, lock yourself in and call for help. He's dangerous, savage. He's a wild beast. He's talking now in beast language. You thought you'd turned him into a man but you were wrong. You've failed. Admit it.

I haven't. He isn't a man yet, but he will be. I've succeeded so far. I'm not going to give up the whole thing now for a pack of yokels.

Fool, she interrupted. He may be hurt. Perhaps he howled like that with pain, and you stand here arguing about him. They may have thrown stones at him. Go and see, quickly.

The body of Virginia, the battle-ground, the quaking instrument, obeyed.

Appius was crouching on the ground, facing the wall, his back to Virginia. His hands were planted in front of him and he was rolling slightly from side to side, balancing from one hand to the other. He was muttering very quickly below his breath now and then breaking out into louder speech, then relapsing again. None of these sounds were words.

Seated as he was, his trousers were hidden from where Virginia stood. She could see only a tousled hairy body, supported on long arms, and a short neck with the head bent almost out of sight, grumbling to the earth.

She was within a few feet of him now. She leant with one hand against a pear trunk. She was very white.

'Appius, are you hurt?'

He seemed not to hear her. Perhaps her voice had been too low and hesitating. She waited again. He seemed not to be hurt. If he were he would still be crying. He was only muttering, quite quietly, to himself; but she thought he was not speaking as he usually did. The muttering was too quick for that, and she couldn't hear any words.

There was only one thing to be done: she must behave as if nothing had happened. She braced herself against the tree and then called him again, more firmly.

'Appius.'

He heard her this time, and turned round, still crouching, moving on his hands. When he saw her he raised his voice and seemed to be explaining to her, but still he didn't speak her language.

She managed to catch his eye. She said very firmly, but smiling at him: 'Come along, darling. Time for tea.'

He looked hard at her, and there was something reproachful in his expression. He was no longer angry, but he went on complaining to her at great length in those sounds of his. His eyes were reproaching her for not understanding him.

This was horrible. He couldn't have become an animal again in so short a time, sitting there and jibbering at her. Didn't he even know what he was doing? Could that rage of his have opened, in some way, channels which her training had so far kept closed to him, so that he had stumbled upon a totally new form of thought and expression? Would he never be able to return?

She must get him back to the house, dress him, set him in his accustomed surroundings. Force of habit would surely make him respond to them. He looked dazed. He must be brought back to himself, and quickly.

'Appius, tea.' She spoke sharply, abruptly, in the tone she used when angry to enforce obedience. The tone seemed to make him think. He had stopped muttering and only looked at her. He seemed to be trying to remember. 'Up, quick.' She took a step towards him, gesticulating. Slowly he got on to his feet and then raised his hands from the ground. But he dropped back on to them. He seemed to be quite dazed.

'Come along. Up, quick. Take mama's hand. Man walk, Appius walk. Come along, now.' She was desperate.

He stood up again and let her take his hand. She brushed the earth from his knickerbockers and pushed the hair back from his eyes.

'Come along now. Appius man. Appius walk.' Her tone was playful. She led him towards the house, talking all the way. 'Appius wants his tea, doesn't he? Appius will be a good boy

110

and wash his hands while mama gets tea, and then he shall have nice jam. Now tell mama whether he doesn't want his tea. Talk to mama, darling.'

He muttered something and then was silent again. She took him into the house, washed his hands and combed his hair; then she lifted him into his chair at the dining-table.

'Oo, what a great boy he is! No good thinking mama can lift him now. He'll have to get used to climbing up by himself.'

She began to pour out the tea.

Appius, left to himself for a moment, looked about him as if he were seeing the room for the first time. He examined the table, the flowers, the portrait of Mr. Hutton on the wall oppose, the plate with the knife laid across it. They seemed to be saying something to him.

'Appius,' he said wonderingly, as Virginia came around the table with his cup. Virginia started and smiled; but she had better take no notice.

'Here's his tea and his bread-and-butter. Now let mama see how nicely he can spread the jam for himself.'

Mechanically he took the spoon from her hand and went through the meal as usual, only, now and then, instead of talking to her as he had done for some time past, he dropped whatever he was holding as if he had forgotten it was there and started to mutter to himself, his eyes wandering vaguely about the room as if he were looking for something. Then he would suddenly see the plate in front of him and go on eating.

'Bad boy,' Virginia scolded gently as she mopped up the tea he had spilt. 'Mustn't drop things like that, or mama will be cross. Now, has he finished?'

He took no notice. He was looking round the room again with that vacant expression. He seemed to hear her only when she spoke sharply, giving an order.

She put her hand on his shoulder now. 'Nursery. Lessons,' she said. The only thing to do was to plunge him as far as possible into the usual routine.

He got up slowly and let her lead him upstairs.

When they got to the nursery she took his jersey from the cupboard. It was not so hot now, and clothes might have a good effect upon him.

'Come along. Let mama put his jersey on.' She arranged it and put on his socks as well, with the sandals on top. Then she waved her hand towards the desk. 'Lessons, Appius. Read.' He sat in the familiar position and found his reading book on the desk in front of him. He opened it at the first page. It was a passage which he had read several times before, but Virginia left him alone.

'Yes?' she said encouragingly.

She held her breath. Would he read as usual, or not? He was blinking hard at the page.

'The dog is the friend of man.'

He had begun. Sentence followed sentence evenly and expressionlessly, in steady procession. Virginia breathed again. She leant back in her chair behind her writing-table in the corner and watched him silently. She would not stop him now whatever mistakes he made.

But he made no mistakes. The familiar look of the print, the absurd illustrations, had reestablished in his brain a connection which had been broken by the shock of his rage. Now he was switched back on to a well-worn track of associations, and the meaningless sentences rolled uninterruptedly from his mouth until he came to the bottom of the page: 'The dog loves man because man feeds and protects him.'

Then there was no more. He had got through the lesson. He had done what mama had told him. Now he could be quiet

112

again and try to think what it was that had made his head swell inside as if it were going to burst, so that he had had to open his mouth to let it out, and it had come out with a huge noise which had frightened him when the swelling had stopped and he could hear it. He couldn't remember how it had begun. There had been a noise, and things waving about, and then redness everywhere and his head swelling and bursting. He muttered to himself, satisfying sounds which meant nothing but made him feel less limp and aching all over.

'Appius. Go on.'

That was mama, speaking sharply to him. She was cross. What did she want?

'Appius, read. Go on.'

Read. There was a book in front of him. Of course. She wanted him to say the marks on it. He bent over the book and began again, blinking: 'The dog is the friend of man.' Once more he went correctly through the first page.

Virginia relaxed for a moment and considered quickly. He had gone on again. Let him read the same page a hundred times over so long as he did read and not stare vacantly and mutter like that to himself. If only she knew what was going on in his mind when he did that. It was so uncanny. Still, he had stopped when she told him to. What would he do, though, when he came to the bottom of the page again? He was almost there.

'The dog loves man because...'

She was just in time.

'...and protects him.'

Swiftly Virginia, standing behind Appius, turned the leaf and shifted the book so that the left-hand page was in line with his eyes. He wavered for a moment and went on. Relieved, she went back to her chair.

113

'That will do,' she said when he had finished the passage. She got up again and closed the book as the last word left his mouth. 'Time for bed.'

She bustled him about, undressed and washed him, had him in bed so quickly that he had had no time to stand and stare. He had only muttered a few times whilst she was bathing him. Then she put out the light and went away, leaving the door slightly open so that she could hear if he moved or called out.

When she was ready for bed herself she went to shut the door and found that he was asleep.

Chapter Fourteen

Appius woke the next morning before Virginia came to him. This scarcely ever happened.

As a rule he would hear her, far off at the top of his tunnel, drawing up the blinds and scraping the ashes from the grate, or, in hot weather, throwing up the window and exclaiming that it was a beautiful day. He would send a little grunt up to her, just to show that he was awake, and then drop back into his warm, ferny nest, though with one ear twitching, until he heard her say: 'Come along. Time to get up!' Then he would slowly open his eyes and see the room golden with sunshine and a pale fire struggling up through its smoke, and jump quickly out of bed into the dressing-gown Virginia was holding ready for him.

But to-day when he first woke there was scarcely any light in the room; only a thin streak of it trickling through the chink between blind and woodwork above his head. The room had a grey, cold look, as if it had been alone for a very long time and nobody was going to live in it any more. It wasn't really cold, but Appius shivered.

To-day he had not woken up gradually, either. Usually there was a gentle sliding upwards into consciousness, comfortable and safe, with little downy scraps of sleep still floating about for him to catch and cling to until he was firmly feet in a sunny world. To-day he had woken abruptly, shot up through a thick layer of sleep with a creaking of wrenched roots, as if he had been pulled suddenly by someone above or pushed hard by something underneath. Before he knew what was happening he found himself with eyes wide open, looking for something in the half light without knowing what it was. His head was raised, peering over the edge of the sheet.

There was nothing there. He curled down again under the blankets and tried to wrap himself back into sleep. He clutched at it all round, but it wouldn't cover him. He looked out again, shivered, and curled up on the other side. It was lonely here without any light, alone with the something which had snatched him awake.

What had done it? What was it he had seen, as he had been torn upwards, lining the walls of the tunnel? Things with pink faces. Waving things. Big mouths making noises. On a wall.

Big, waving noises.

'Ape,' they were saying. 'Ape, ape, ape.'

As he said it in his mind, his mind gave a great snarl, but by the time it had got to his mouth it was only a little sleepy grunt. He could feel the hair stirring prickily along the back of his neck.

When his mind had stopped snarling he said it aloud; 'Ape.' What was it? Why did it pull a red sheet across his eyes and give him a tickly feeling down his back? Did it mean anything? What did it mean? He must ask mama.

Why didn't mama come?

'Ape, ape.' The waving noises had big mouths and the

116

mouths were waving red noises at him; red mouths waving big noises. They wouldn't stop. They were all round the mouth of his tunnel so that he couldn't get back into it. Why didn't mama come and drive them away? No mama.

He tossed from side to side under the clothes, curling more tightly, stretching, rolling on his back, on his face, dragging the clothes with him each time he turned until they were all humped up in the middle of the bed and cold wind was coming in at the sides. Mama waving big noises. Big mouths drive away mama. His toes were tangled up in the sheet. His nails scraped against it and one got caught. He dragged it away, whimpering. His back was cold.

He tossed and fretted. Mama wave red mouths. Drive away big noises.

Down to the bottom of the bed. There was some blanket there. He rolled right underneath it and his back got warm, but he couldn't breathe.

He spluttered and came up again; shivered as he met the air.

'Well. What a mess he's got himself into.'

There was mama at last. He must tell her to drive away red noises. He opened his eyes, which had been screwed tight shut, and blinked. The room was light now, although mama hadn't drawn up the blinds yet.

'Noises, mama…'

He spluttered. He found that after all he couldn't tell her about the noises. What was it he wanted to say about them? Now it was light he couldn't quite remember. They were red and waving and there were mouths and pink faces. But what was waving, the mouths or the faces? And what was red? The faces? No, they were pink.

It had all got mixed up. He would never be able to make

117

her understand. He began to whimper. He put out a hand and caught at her dress. It was made of thin, white stuff, neither rough nor slippery. It felt safe.

'What is it, darling? Tell mama all about it.'

She sat on the edge of the bed and drew him towards her. He snuggled against her in the hollow of her arm and thought hard, looking fixedly up at the blind which the sunlight had made bright yellow.

What was it about noises and faces and redness? He couldn't get it straight, and somehow it didn't matter so much now. Mama was warm and safe-feeling through the thin frock. He liked the faint bump-bump she made up against his shoulder and the firm pressure of her arm around his middle. The noises really didn't matter. Only he'd wanted to tell her...

That was it. Ape, ape. What was it? He thought deeply.

'What is it, darling? Tell mama.' Her voice was soft to-day, and secure.

He struggled: 'Ape. What? Noises, ape, ape. Ape what?'

She understood.

'What is "ape", darling? Why, nothing. They were bad boys. They didn't mean anything.'

He frowned. It must mean something, or he wouldn't have to keep puzzling about it.

But she was speaking again: 'Ape is a kind of animal, that's all.'

'Ape, animal.' He considered.

She corrected him gently: 'One kind of animal, dear. Dog animal, horse animal, ape animal. You see?'

He pondered: 'Ape one animal.'

That was all right. But why did the noises say 'ape,' and why was it such a horrid word? How could he ask that?

'Noises,' he began. 'Noises say ape. Ape one animal. Noises

say one animal. What? Noises what? Say ape. What?' He floundered hopelessly.

She helped him out: 'Did the voices say "ape"? Is that it?' She searched frantically for an explanation. 'The noises were boys,' she began, to gain time.

'Boys? Appius boy.'

'Yes, darling. But Appius is a good boy. Noises bad boys. Good boys don't say "ape". There. Now Appius knows all about it, and it's quite time he got up. Dressing-gown, quick.' Hurriedly she got him out of bed. He seemed to be satisfied, but if he were left alone to think he might discover that he didn't understand after all.

She handed him his slippers. While he put them on she pulled up the blinds, and a dazzling light broke into the room, making her blink almost as much as Appius. Her eyes were tired and her face drawn, for she had slept no more than he, but her voice was bright and she was smiling as she hurried him through his washing and dressing and got him to the breakfast table.

She must give him plenty to do so that he had no time to think. At least he had found his tongue during the night. She need not have spent sleepless hours on that account. His mind seemed brighter than ever this morning. Almost too bright.

She glanced at him gravely eating his porridge and wondered what he was thinking about now.

In a moment he told her: 'Appius man,' he said thickly, through the porridge. 'Appius kill bad boys.'

She started but smiled quickly. He seemed quite calm and satisfied. So long as he had forgotten the ape problem all was well.

'Yes, darling. Appius kill bad boys. That's right.'

They would certainly not come back, she thought. They

must have had enough of a fright. Besides, she would have the wall heavily spiked at once.

Appius went on eating contentedly.

The most annoying thing, she thought as she sipped her tea, was that he would have to see the wall again. He couldn't be kept away, permanently, from that part of the garden. In time he might, of course, forget yesterday altogether. But she doubted that. He had a very good memory. And even supposing he forgot it, if he should suddenly find himself face to face with that piece of wall he might remember, and the affair would be started all over again. Something she had heard about remounting a horse immediately after a fall recurred to her as she sipped. He had better face the wall again at once; see it with her and find out that it didn't hurt him. Then he would be all right. At any rate it was worth trying.

'Finished, darling?' She eyed him anxiously.

'Then come along in the garden with mama.'

Taking his hand firmly in hers, she walked him slowly down the side path which he had taken the day before, stopping now and then, as she always did, to pick off a withered rose or a sweet-pea gone to seed, or to tighten the bass of a plant which was breaking away from its stake. She talked to him meanwhile, keeping his attention as far as possible from the direction they were taking.

'Look at that bird over there. The bird is looking for a worm. There, look. He's caught it. How greedy he is; a whole worm at one mouthful. Appius isn't greedy like that, is he?' As they came to the turn in the path she felt Appius's hand twitch in hers and knew that he had begun to think. It was time to tackle the subject boldly.

'Only bad boys are greedy like the bird we saw just now,' she began. 'Bad boys who make noises. But they won't make noises any more. Mama won't let them. Mama is very, very cross with them, and won't let them come any more.' They were nearing the danger point. Virginia felt Appius shrink towards her. His eyes were taking on a vacant expression and seemed to have sunk further into his head, while his neck had almost disappeared. Suddenly she noticed, sticking in the ground under a tree, the spade which Appius had left there the day before. It saved her.

'Look!' she cried. 'Spade! Man digs the earth. Come along, darling. Appius dig. Appius man.'

He hesitated.

'Appius big man,' she urged. 'Appius kill bad boys. Bad boys can't dig the earth, but Appius can. Appius man. Appius digs the earth.'

She had led him right up to the spade, now. Suddenly he broke away from her hand and rushed upon it. He sent it deep into the ground, turning up an enormous clod of matted roots and leaf-mould.

His face cleared. He flung the clod, with his whole strength, smack against the wall which had held the voices. The wall didn't answer. It was killed. There were brown bits of mould sticking to it, all over, where he had hit it, and it didn't make any noise at all.

'Appius man!' he shouted fiercely.

Virginia smiled.

Chapter Fifteen

Virginia had sent Appius to play in the nursery while she cleared the breakfast table.

She dared not leave him alone in the garden just yet. All the same, it was wonderful how he had seemed to overcome his fear of the wall just now. What a blessing the spade had been there. It had saved the situation. If it hadn't been for that and his fondness for digging he might have gone on for ages brooding about the voices and the wall, and developed a permanent fear of that end of the garden. She remembered that something like that had happened after his fall from the pear tree. For weeks afterwards she hadn't been able to get him to play near the trees. Anyway, that had cured him of climbing, she thought. That had been ages ago, when he was quite tiny, and of course he had forgotten his fear of the trees after a time, but he had never tried to climb them since.

She remembered so well his falling and rolling at her feet, kicking and scratching, and how sulky he had been all day afterwards. It had been a summer's day, like this, but earlier in the year; the pear trees had been in bloom, and Appius had shaken off so much of the blossom that they had had very few pears that year. It seemed like yesterday; but to him of course, it was nearly a lifetime, much further back than he could remember.

Three years ago, that was; and now Appius was nearly six. Six years since she came to the cottage. She had almost forgotten the look of the outside world; she hadn't been able to leave Appius for a single day. Not that she regretted it for a moment. Did the ladies' residential club still exist at Earl's Court?—she wondered. Did they still sip coffee in the lounge, on creaking wicker chairs with blue borders? Or had the wicker chairs fallen to pieces long ago?

She swept up the crumbs and carried the piled tray of crockery out to the scullery.

While she waited for the water to boil she stood with folded arms and stared out at the dusty ivy on the wall beyond the window. Cobwebs filmed the dingy green of the old leaves and choked with their linked threads the young shoots. Lumps of broken web clung to the new, small leaves and dangled from them, limp and aimless.

What was Appius doing overhead? He seemed to be moving about a lot. Only playing. He was dragging something or other.

Those children yesterday. What could she do about it? Send a complaint to the village school, perhaps. Disgusting. Filthy little brutes. Kicking their heels on her wall and daring to shout at Appius. A pity he couldn't reach them. Ape, indeed.

She flushed with annoyance.

As if he weren't a hundred times more civilised than they were. Clean and sweet in his little linen knickers, digging away as good as gold. Dear little fellow. And those hulking, coarse

123

brutes must shout at him just because he had a bit more hair on his chest than they had. And a great deal more brains in his head, too. Disgusting. She'd write to the schoolmaster at once.

The kettle was boiling over, the spilled water sizzling on the stove. Her lips pursed, she emptied the kettle and did the washing-up, carrying the clean china from the sink to the cupboard with a precise, indignant step, a quick, metallic tap-tap on the tiled floor.

That was done. Now she could go and see what Appius was doing. She hadn't taken the cloth off the table, though.

She went back to the dining-room and removed the cloth. As she stood folding it the residential club came again into her mind. Did they still have sole and creme caramel four nights a week: two square inches of tired nameless fish and a spoonful of sour custard? She didn't feed Appius like that, she thought with satisfaction.

And the flower-sellers around Earl's Court station: did they still haul their heavy baskets or wheel their trucks across the road every five minutes, splashing strange dabs of colour against the grimy brick buildings? Great moving banks of tulips or mimosa or chrysanthemums.

Why did people buy more flowers at Earl's Court than in any other district of London? Because of the bed-sitting-rooms there. It sounded like the answer to a riddle. The bed-sitting-room women tried to give reality to their unreal, meaningless dwellings with a slim vase of tulips or mimosa; just as they put 'fireside chairs' by their hired gas stoves among the salvage from some country rectory. People bought flowers in Piccadilly or Trafalgar Square because they were going home. At Earl's Court they bought flowers because they had no home to go to.

She slipped the folded cloth into a sideboard drawer and

clicked the drawer to. Then she replaced the bowl of roses in the centre of the table and went upstairs to the nursery. What could Appius be doing? He was making no noise now. She opened the door quietly.

Not a sound in the room. The first thing she saw was the broken toy train overturned and neglected in the middle of the floor. Where was Appius? She looked around the room in amazement. Everything was in order except for the derelict engine and the unmade bed. The thought shot across her mind: I've forgotten to make it. But: 'Appius, where are you?' Her heart missed a beat.

There was a movement of the curtain above the bed as if something huddled on the window sill behind it had turned round.

'Appius, darling! Whatever is he doing there? What a fright he gave mama.'

He was crouching on the sill with the curtain drawn around him, head lowered and shoulders raised: a small bundle of despondency staring out across the garden.

'Why, darling, what is it? Why isn't he playing? Why is he sitting up there and looking so miserable all by himself? Did mama leave him alone, then?'

She was sitting on the unmade bed, clasping him in her arms. She looked at him anxiously. Could he be ill? She couldn't see that anything was wrong with him. But he had been strange and silent ever since that wretched business yesterday.

'Tell mama, then.' She smoothed back his hair and tickled him gently behind the car. 'Did nasty mama leave him to play all by himself? Or wouldn't the naughty engine play with him? Tell mama all about it, pet.'

His face was turned away from her. She bent over to look at

it. His lids were blinking slowly and his mouth twitched now and then. He was still staring up at the window. If only he would look at her and tell her what was the matter. She turned his face round gently with one hand while the other held him tightly against her.

'Talk to mama, there's a good boy.'

'Bad boys,' he said slowly, as if her words had prompted him. 'Bad boys say ape. Why? Why bad boys?' He shivered.

'Oh!' She pressed his head against her shoulder and rocked him to and fro. 'Why, darling, you're not worrying still about the boys, surely. They're *bad* boys, bad, bad, bad boys. Appius mustn't think about them any more. Why, mama's own darling boy, they aren't worth one thought of your little head.'

But she knew that he didn't understand her.

'Now listen. Bad boys will never come any more, never. Bad boys are dead. Mama has killed them so that they'll never bother Appius again. Bad boys dead, dead.'

He looked around at her, his face brightening.

'Bad boys dead. Mama kill bad boys.' Slowly the idea penetrated. 'Bad boys dead. Mama kill boys. Boys not come. Mama good. Bad boys dead.' He was happy now, but not so lively as usual, and he was shivering again.

'Yes, darling.'

She smiled at him, stroking his neck thoughtfully with one finger. He really couldn't be well or he wouldn't brood and worry like this, and he ought not to be so cold. Better put him to bed for a bit and then see how he was. She lifted him right on to her lap and held him there while she arranged the tumbled bedclothes with her free hand.

'Now listen.' She was rocking him again. 'Appius is going to sleep in a nice warm bed, and mama will come and sit with him all the time, and then when he wakes up she'll play with him. Only he must be good first and stay in bed while she gets him his hot bottle.'

She undressed him and tucked him in. He seemed not to mind, but lay there and looked at her silently while she spread the eiderdown. Then she stooped suddenly and clutched him to her, blanket and all.

'Mama's own baby. He won't ever be frightened any more, will he? Mama won't let anyone hurt him, ever.' She kissed his head lightly and smoothed the sheet. 'Now mama will go and fetch his bottle, and he must be good, remember.' She raised a finger warningly and went out.

In the scullery she lit the gas under a kettle and raked the cupboard for his hot water bottle.

What would she do if he were really ill? She had nobody to send for a doctor. Besides, the village doctor was probably useless. She'd have to get one from town. Wire? Send a telegram by the next tradesman who came? She couldn't leave Appius alone if he were ill. Then she thought suddenly: supposing no doctor would come. Supposing if one did come he would do nothing for Appius because he wasn't an ordinary child. What could she do then? Send for a vet? She winced as if the scalding water had touched her. She would look after him herself; she knew enough medicine for that. Her determination in itself would cure him. She wouldn't leave him for a moment, day or night. She would force him to be well with all the will that was in her.

There. His bottle was ready. She must take it up now and see that he hadn't got out of bed after she had left him. Probably he'd only caught a slight chill from playing in the heat and then coming into the cool dining-room. She should have remembered to see that he put his coat on when he came in.

As she was leaving the scullery the door-bell rang loudly. A tradesman's boy. Should she send him for a doctor? No. She'd see first whether it were necessary. The bottle still in her hand, she opened the door.

'Inspector, mum.' The man touched his helmet.

Police! Whatever did he want? She watched him impatiently as he fumbled among a sheaf of notes.

'Miss 'Utton?'

'Yes.' Her tone was sharp. Couldn't he hurry up? The bottle would get cold while she was standing here by the open door. She pushed it under her arm.

He looked up from the notes, embarrassed, still fumbling. 'Er. We was told at the station as 'ow you 'ad a dangerous pet 'ere. Er.'

She interrupted him: 'Pet? Certainly not. I keep no pets.' Her voice was like a knife cutting through his lumbering rustic speech. At the word 'pet' she felt a faint shiver run down her spine. The man must be put in his place. 'No pets at all. Good morning.' She began to shut the door.

"Ere. 'Alf a minute, mum. You'll excuse me, but we was told as 'ow some children was roared at by a ape on your premises. Savage, it were. Now as you knows, mum…'

'I have told you I keep no pets.'

The man was shuffling with his notes again, stopping to push back his helmet and wipe his face. It was very red and hot and round, like a red, shiny egg. She looked at him with distaste, noticing how his neck bulged over his uniform collar. The collar was greasy at the edge.

'At ten-thirty on the mornin'…'

Would he never go?

'I have told you that I have no pets whatever. It is no concern of mine what tales the village children may bring to the station. I have frequently had cause to complain of the

128

noise they make under the windows and the damage they do to the wall. I should be glad if the police could do something to remedy this. As for pets, I have told you I have none. I live here with my adopted son, and we are quite alone.'

'No pets. Lives with adopted son. Was informed on calling at the residence of Miss 'Utton at twelve noon…' The man had a grimy pencil-stub clutched in his fist. Painfully he found a blank page among his notes and wrote, supporting the paper against the door-post. His mouth framed the words. 'At twelve noon on the twenty-third inst…'

'Good morning.' This time Virginia shut the door. Clutching the bottle triumphantly, she ran upstairs.

Up on the landing she stopped suddenly. That was absurd, shutting the door on him like that. Stupid to put the police against her.

She hesitated. Go down and say something more? What could she say? Only make him suspicious. Besides, he would have gone by this time. She shrugged her shoulders. Do him good. Talking about pets. *Pets*. Her face burned with indignation.

Appius was lying in bed as she had left him, his eyes open. 'Has mama been very long, then?'

She tucked the bottle down beside him. He put out a hand, and in a moment had curled up beside the bottle, one arm thrown over it. His lids were drooping heavily.

Let him sleep. That would be the best thing for him. Quietly she drew the blind above the bed and went over to the farther window. His eyes were shut now. She drew the second blind and sat down behind her table in the dim light.

Let him sleep. Probably he had not slept the night before; he had been excited and upset. When he woke he would be all right. His nerves quietened by the rest, he would forget about yesterday's scene in the garden.

That policeman, though. Would he come back? If so, what should she do?

She passed a hand across her forehead, under her hair. The hand was cool, it helped her to think. She put up the other and leant her head on them, elbows on the table. She could feel her eyes throbbing against her palms through their closed lids.

Had she been wrong to send him away like that? Perhaps she ought to have let him come in and see for himself; shown him Appius ill in bed. Perhaps he would have been satisfied then, she thought bitterly. Pets. She almost laughed. An absurd name, pets. Known only to the police and to landladies. No children or pets allowed. Pets. Canaries and Pekinese. Did any owner of a decent dog describe it as a pet? Would the policeman have called Appius a pet if he had seen him?

How hot her eyes were. The darkness of her hands was comforting. The room was cool too, with the blinds drawn, and very quiet. There wasn't a sound except for a bee buzzing outside the blind, and Appius's low regular breathing. He was asleep now.

I live here with my adopted son. That had been clever. She had been surprised when she had heard her voice saying it. And it was true, too. She had never so far stopped to define their relationship, but the policeman's stupidity had called out the definition in a moment. My adopted son. We live here alone. No children or pets allowed. My adopted son.

The buzzing had grown louder. It seemed to fill the room. Ze-oo, ze-oo. It was cool, pressing against her burning lids. They were so heavy. They were sinking into the buzzing, into the silence. The buzzing was dying away in the distance; it was only a purring in the stillness. Zee-ooo.

Virginia slept, her head sunk upon the table. The darkened

room was very quiet, except for the bees still drumming against the yellow blind, outside in the sunshine.

'Mama. Appius want tea.'

Virginia jumped.

'Yes, darling?'

What had he said? Had she been asleep? How light the room was, and yet the blinds were drawn. She pressed her finger-tips against her eye-lids.

'What is it, darling? What does Appius want?'

He was sitting up in bed, pulling at the eiderdown.

'Tea?' She looked at her watch. Four. Had she slept for over three hours? 'Yes, of course he shall have his tea. Mama was asleep.' She got up unsteadily and smiled at him, feeling that her mouth was twisted. Its roof was dry, and she had a dull, muffled ache in her head as if her heart were beating under her temples. She jerked the blinds, which flew up with a click.

Appius was jumping up and down under the clothes. 'Appius want tea. Appius want get up.' He wasn't ill, at least.

'Very well, he can get up.' She tried to make her voice brisk, but she could feel the words falling limply from her tongue. 'He can try to dress himself while mama gets the tea and brings it up here.'

She handed him his clothes and went downstairs again.

Chapter Sixteen

Appius was seven years old. It was early November, the time of year at which he had come to the cottage. He stood now at the nursery window, gazing absently across the sodden lawn at a file of yellow daisies staggering along by the side wall. His eyes followed their wobbling line to the bottom of the garden and stared without interest at patches of brownish red brick connecting the bare arms of the pear trees. It was more than a year since the village boys had climbed there and shouted at him.

Toys, a new clockwork train and regiment of lead soldiers, were stacked neatly beside the coal-box, but Appius was not playing. It was time for lessons. He stood squarely in front of the window, for now he could just see over the sill without climbing or hanging by his hands, and spoke quietly: 'Mama come, Appius do lessons. Appius get book.' He went over to the bookcase and considered the higher shelves.

At first, when he was small, the bottom shelf only had been filled, by the London firm which supplied the furniture, with children's books and picture alphabets. Gradually Virginia had stocked the second with primers and simple reading books, and now all three shelves were full; the highest, just on a level with his eyes, held first histories and geographies and some elementary arithmetics with the leaves still uncut.

Appius looked along this top rank until he came to a red book with heavy black lettering: First Lessons In History. This he took out. 'History book, Mama come, Appius read history.' He carried it over to the desk and, sitting down, turned the leaves meditatively.

'King Alfred. King Alfred great man. King Alfred burn cakes. Burn cakes bad. Appius not burn cakes. Appius more great man.' He turned the page. 'Canute. Canute great man. Canute tell sea stop. Appius tell soldiers stand. Soldiers stand.' Over again. 'Henry.'

He frowned. Two straight lines standing up with a line lying on top and another underneath. What did that spell?

'Second. Henry-Second. Henry-Second great man. Henry-Second not smile. Smile, pull mouth.' He put his fingers in the corner of his mouth and pulled it sideways until it was underneath his ear. Then the other side. Then he released it. 'Mama smile. Appius not smile. Appius great man.'

He turned another page. 'King…' He looked more closely. 'King… Appius not read King.' He pushed the book away and went over to the fire.

'Why mama not come?'

Noticing the lead soldiers standing patiently by the coal-box, he picked them up one at a time.

'King-Alfred stand. Canute stand. Henry-Second stand.' He set them in a row leaning against the fender and stood in front of them with arms folded. 'King-Alfred great man. Canute great man. Henry-Second great man. Appius more great man.' He scowled at them from under his brows. Then he raised his head and listened.

'Mama come.'

She was crossing the hall, coming up the stairs, along the passage.

'Mama. Appius read history.'

'Yes, darling. Appius shall read history. But Appius will have to learn to read by himself when mama isn't here.'

She sat down, a little breathless with haste, smiling to herself. She had known he would be impatient. He was so keen on his lessons now, and so proud of his progress, that she could hardly get him to play.

'Very well, begin. Mama is ready.'

But Appius was shuffling the leaves of his book. He looked up at her. 'Appius read history,' he repeated.

'Yes, yes. Begin.'

He frowned.

'Appius *read* history. Mama not come. Appius read history. King-Alfred, Canute, Henry-Second.'

'Oh, I see. Appius has read history to himself. Well?'

How she wished she could make him speak grammatically. It was strange that he should take an interest in history and yet seem incapable of understanding a simple grammatical construction. Of course, she wasn't a trained teacher, she reflected. It seemed that she couldn't explain it properly. She would really have to get him a tutor soon. After all, a boy needed a man to teach him.

'Well?' she repeated.

'King-Alfred, Canute, Henry-Second, great man.' He paused.

'Great men,' she corrected.

'Great man,' he insisted. 'Have world. *What*, world?'

'What is the world?' She was surprised. 'Why, I told you

134

ages ago. The world is everything.' She swept her arm around. 'The world is the room and the house and the garden and everything beyond. The world is round,' she added.

'Round?'

He was obviously puzzled. Suddenly she had an idea. 'If Appius will be good and wait, mama will show him what the world is like. He can go on reading his book.'

She hurried along the passage to her own room. She had noticed it only the other day: an old globe which had stood in her father's study and had been pushed into a trunk with a few things of his she had not cared to sell when the vicarage was given up. They had been left undisturbed ever since.

She supported the creaking lid with one hand and rummaged with the other: his cassock and hood, a pipe-rack, an antique duelling pistol of his father's, a pair of gloves, some manuscript sermons, a heavy clock which had stood on his study mantelpiece, and the globe. She dusted it hastily with a comer of the cassock and dropped the lid.

In the nursery she stood the globe on her table and called Appius. 'Look. Here is the world. Now Appius can see for himself what it's like.'

'World? That?' He pointed, and blinked wonderingly. 'World?'

He seized it with both hands and lifted it from the table. It was a round ball, green and blue in patches, with brown splashes on the green, and a metal frame around it ending in a black wooden stand. 'World?'

'Yes, dear.'

Then she noticed his hands as they held the globe, exploring the grooved contours of the stand. 'Oh, Appius. Your sleeves!'

His hands, all but the fingers, were hidden under turned down jersey cuffs which hung limply over the thin knuckles,

135

showing a thick ridge of seam.

'Darling, you really are very naughty. How often have I told you to turn back your cuffs on your wrists when you put on the jersey? Come here and let me do it.'

She arranged the cuffs, giving each hand a little slap as she finished. Why was he so careless about details? He had learnt to dress himself at last, but he was for ever appearing with his shoe-laces untied, or cuffs over his hands, or braces trailing on the floor. Such bad training for his character. She had made this jersey herself because those she bought were always too short in the sleeve and too tight in the neck, and yet he couldn't take the trouble to put it on properly. She sighed a little. Perhaps it was because he was so clever that he didn't notice things like this. It was astonishing sometimes how quickly he would pick up an idea and meditate about it for days afterwards. How really bright he was at times. This interest, now, in the shape of the earth; quite remarkable in a child of seven. She straightened his collar and turned briskly to the globe.

'Yes, dear. This is the earth, the world. These green patches are countries and the blue are seas. Now this is England, where we are.'

She made the globe revolve in Appius's hands, for he had pounced upon it as soon as she had released him.

'Here is England, an island with sea all around it. "An island is a piece of land entirely surrounded by water"—you remember? And these big pieces of land are called continents. That's a new name for Appius to learn, isn't it?'

Appius was studying the globe intently, feeling it all over. 'World? This world?' He was still incredulous.

'Yes, this is the world. Now each of these continents has a different name, Europe, Asia, Africa'—she touched them

136

with her finger— 'and the rest. Each has a different kind of weather and different kinds of plants and animals, and each has the sea around it, where the blue is. Now Appius knows all about the sea. It's made of water and has fish swimming in it, and big boats sailing on it.'

'World, this?' His voice was no longer incredulous, but eager.

How intelligent he was, taking in all she could tell him, and feeling the mystery and attraction of new things. He really wanted to learn; she could tell by his eyes what an interest he was taking. That was a fine idea of hers, remembering the old globe. It seemed to appeal to his imagination better than maps.

'World. Great man has world.'

Funny child. Strange what an interest he took in humanity. Surely that was a good sign. He found it far more fascinating than nature study, she fancied. He preferred history to geography, too, as a rule. His eyes were shining now with triumph at his connection of the two.

'Yes, dear. Great men rule the world. The great men you read about in your history book have ruled it, or parts of it.'

How excited he was.

'Great man has world. Appius has world. Appius, *world*!' He jumped up and down, hugging the globe to him. Then he turned to the three lead soldiers still drawn up by the fender. 'King-Alfred, Canute, Henry-Second,' he addressed them sternly, 'Appius has *world*. Appius *more* great man.' He strutted backwards and forwards in front of them, rolling the globe against his chest.

Virginia laughed and put out a hand to catch his arm.

'Oh, darling, how funny you are! Of course, you know that this isn't really the world, this globe. It's a picture of it, like the pictures in the history book, only it's made solid instead of being drawn on paper. That is called sculpture, when things are made instead of being drawn. One day you'll learn all about it. You see, this isn't really Canute sitting on the seashore, is it? It's a picture of him. Well, this is a picture of the world. The real world is far too big for Appius to hold. Why, he's walking on it all the time.'

All the same, she thought, it's a symbol, perhaps. Perhaps he knows that he will own the world some day.

Appius blinked at her, tears gathering in his eyes.

'World,' he said crossly, as she tried to take the globe from him. 'Appius has world.' He jerked it out of her reach and she had to let him keep it.

'No, darling,' she explained patiently. 'This,' touching the globe, 'is a picture of the world. Picture. Look, this is a picture of Canute. Not Canute, but a picture of Canute. Now this is a picture of the world. Not the world, but a picture of the world.'

Slowly he blinked-in the idea 'Not world.' His tone was disgusted; he hurled the globe on to the floor. 'Appius want world.'

Virginia picked up the globe and examined a crack on its surface.

'Listen.' She set the globe on the side of the table farther from him, but he was taking no more interest in it.

'Listen. This is a picture of the world. The real world is just like this but very big. Big.' She stretched her arms as far as they would go and curved them. 'The world is much, much bigger. But Appius can conquer the world, perhaps, one day, when he's a big man. Only he'll have to work hard and fight with his brain. Brain, little Appius.'

She thought for a moment.

'You see, dear, the world is all around Appius and under

138

his feet.' She pointed to the floor and then out of the window. 'Every time Appius walks, in here or out in the garden, he is walking on the world.'

She paused. Appius had stopped listening. He was considering hard.

'Picture world,' he said. 'World more big. *World*.' He pointed downwards. 'Appius get world.'

He seemed more cheerful now. He went over to the soldiers and glared at them, with arms folded.

'King Alfred, Canute, Henry-Second,' he said. 'World more big. Appius more great man. Appius get world.' He turned to Virginia. 'Appius want dig.'

She raised her eyebrows.

'Want to go in the garden, dear? Tired already? Well, I expect you can. It's stopped raining. But you must have your coat and heavy shoes on.'

She dressed him and sent him out. 'Run along, then. Mama will come in a minute.' How strange, she thought when he had gone. He had seemed so much interested, and then suddenly he had wanted to go out and play. All children were like that, she supposed. They got tired all at once, and restless. After all, he was wonderfully good for his age. Evidently he had been reading to himself before she came in, and now he had been working hard, trying to take in all she had told him. Well, she'd better go and see that he wasn't getting his feet wet.

From the window she could see his short, sturdy figure frantically turning up an empty patch of soil.

Chapter Seventeen

I'm not so young as I was, Virginia was thinking.

She had been making her bed, and on her way out of the room had stopped in front of the dressing-table to poke her hair into place with a pin. Bending forwards, she examined her face more closely. Plenty of small wrinkles. Not a double chin; she was too thin for that, luckily, but her skin looked tired and so did her hair. It fell in a pale flat cake on either side of her head, covering her ears. Her eyebrows, too, which had never been strongly marked, had grown thinner lately. Seven and a half years of housework had set their mark upon her neglected skin as well as upon her roughened hands. Responsibility for Appius had drawn lines at the corners of her mouth. It had also brought expression into the light, opaque eyes, but at the moment they showed only personal anxiety under the raw spring light which poured full upon her from the open window.

Was she really so old as that? It was months since she had had time to notice her appearance. In the morning there was Appius to be got up and the fires to be laid and breakfast to be prepared, and at night she was too tired for more than a perfunctory stroke of the brush and a quick clamber into bed. She couldn't remember consciously looking at herself since one day, years ago, when she had been wondering how she would look to Appius's school-fellows, and whether she could do him credit. She had thought then that she might still look young at times, though that, of course, was by artificial light. But she would have more time to attend to herself as he grew older. The first few years were always trying.

That had been when Appius was just learning to read, and now he was doing history and geography and getting ready for a tutor in the autumn. She would try all the agencies and insist upon having a really capable man, neither too old nor too young: somebody sympathetic and genuinely fond of children, who would be a companion to him sometimes and teach him to play cricket on the lawn as well as grounding him thoroughly in grammar and arithmetic. He had better not be resident; that would interfere too much with their home life, the intimacy of mother and son. Besides, there was no room in the cottage. She could find him some nice lodgings in the village, and then she and Appius could still have their evenings and Sundays alone together.

While she thought, she was mechanically tidying the dressing-table, shaking the lace mats, emptying the wickerwork toilet-tidy out of the window, polishing the plated pin-tray on the back of her hand.

There was Appius coming out of the nursery. What was he doing? She called him: 'Appius, darling. Are you going out? Have you got your warm coat on?'

She heard him stop in the passage.

'Mama?'

'Come here, darling. Mama's room. What does Appius

141

want?'

She heard him take a few steps and stop again as if he were puzzled. She remembered. Of course, he had never been in her room. She hardly entered it herself in the daytime. Going to the door, she beckoned to him.

'Appius go play garden,' he explained.

'Very well, dear. Come here and let mama see how he's dressed. Come and see mama's room. He's never seen it, has he?'

She drew him in and examined him critically. 'Why, he hasn't even got a coat on. He doesn't think he's going out like that, does he? A nice cold he'd get. Wait a minute while mama puts these things straight, and she'll see to him.'

She picked up the brushes, comb and back-glass, which she had dropped on the bed, and arranged them on the dressing-table. As she set them neatly in place, glass in the middle, comb to the right, brush to the left and clothes-brush perpendicular along the top, she heard a sudden cry from Appius: 'Mama!'

It was frightened, appealing. In a moment she was at his side.

'Appius, darling, what is it?'

He was cowering against the side of the bed. What on earth was the matter with him? Then she followed his eyes and laughed. Of course! He was seeing himself in the long mirror of the wardrobe; seeing himself probably for the first time, since there was no mirror in the nursery.

'Yes. Just look what a big boy Appius is! Why, darling, there's nothing to be afraid of.'

But Appius was almost crying. 'Boy. Bad boy in cupboard.' He shrank against her and hid his face.

She soothed him with her voice, holding him against her and stroking his head. 'No bad boy, darling. You've forgotten

142

that mama killed all the bad boys ages ago. No bad boy in cupboard. Nobody will hurt Appius. Look up, darling, and mama will show him there's nothing there, only a picture of Appius himself. Now we'll make it a picture of mama. Just look. Look at the picture of mama.'

When he had stopped crying she turned him round and stood a little away from him where she was reflected in the mirror. 'Look, Appius. Look at mama. Look at mama's picture.'

Unwillingly he followed her hand which was pointing at the cupboard where the bad boy was hidden. There was mama instead. But mama was beside him! Two mamas!

He began to cry. But the mama who was nearer had put an arm around him and was holding his head against her so that he couldn't see the other.

'Silly boy,' she was saying. 'That's only a picture of mama, just like the pictures in the book. See? Now look at a picture of Appius. Doesn't Appius want to see his own picture? Of course he does. Now look. Instead of a picture of mama he'll see a picture of Appius. Look.'

She turned him round gently, with her arm still over his shoulders. He looked unwillingly from under his lids. Then he lifted them and looked, wide-eyed. A picture of mama and... 'Appius?' He pointed doubtfully. The picture pointed too. He dropped his hand, doubtful and suspicious.

She wouldn't give him time to be afraid. 'See. Mama holds Appius's hand. Now the picture of mama holds Appius's hand. Don't be afraid, darling. There's nobody there.'

She opened the cupboard and showed him clothes neatly stacked on shelves. She closed it again, and the picture of Appius was there with mama looking at him.

'Appius?' He was getting used to the idea. 'Appius.'

He pointed. So did the picture. Yes, it was his, after all.

He examined it with interest. It hadn't struck him before that he might have a picture like Canute and Henry-Second and the others: King-John who wrote his name, and Richardthelionheart who killed Saracens, who were a kind of men. But he had. And it was bigger than theirs, too. Theirs only filled half a page each in the history book, while his filled a great big cupboard. He folded his arms and looked at it.

'Appius great man,' he said. 'Appius *more* great man.'

Virginia smiled and stood back to be out of the picture. Let him find himself.

He unfolded his arms and put his hands in his pockets. So did the picture. Yes, it was his picture. It did what he did.

For some time he considered himself in silence: the short stocky figure in its red jersey suit; the long arms and broad, rather protruding chest; the large head with wide, forward-set mouth and tiny nose and behind them two dark, bright, interested eyes; hair parted above them, and two small, pink ears just showing around the corners. 'Appius great, great man,' he decided.

Virginia laughed happily and came and stood beside him, an arm over his shoulders.

'Now look at Appius and mama together. See what a big boy Appius is. Nearly as tall as mama.'

He reached not quite to her shoulder, short as she was, but she bent her knees slightly to make him appear taller.

The picture pleased her. Her spare figure looked quite frail beside his heavy frame. When he had grown a little taller he would be all that a son should be, fine and strong, able to protect her when she grew still more frail with age. The picture of a mother and her big son.

She realised that Appius was shuffling his feet. Briskly she broke up the group. 'Come along. Appius mustn't admire himself all day! He's going to play in the garden, isn't he? Mama will find him his coat and scarf so that he doesn't get cold. He must take care of himself so that he'll grow into a big, strong man and look after mama when she's an old, old woman.'

She patted his shoulder playfully and guided him towards the door.

Chapter Eighteen

'Flowers, why?'

Appius looked up from Second Lessons in History and held out the book to Virginia.

'Flowers.' He pointed to a bowl of crimson peonies which stood on the nursery window-sill, then back to the picture on the open page.

It was summer again. All this year, in the intervals of digging, which in the hope of discovering the world he had taken up with renewed ardour, and of admiring his picture in mama's room, Appius had been studying the habits of great men. He had observed Swalter-Raleigh put his coat on the ground in front of a mama, and heard Philip-Sidney say 'Philip-Sidney want. Man more want.' (Philip-Sidney not want. Philip-Sidney great man.) He had watched great men fight and kill and ride horses, and stand and talk, with one hand stuck in the front of their coats, but now here was a great man lying flat in a box with flowers all over him.

'Man lie,' he explained, sliding from his chair on to the floor and lying there, arms outstretched. 'Flowers on man.'

He indicated the peonies on the window-sill and made the gesture of strewing them on his chest.

'Get up, Appius, and bring me the book.' She took it from him. 'Burial of Napoleon? Why, you see, he's dead. When people are dead other people put flowers on them because they are sorry they are dead.'

'Dead? Flowers?'

'No, the men are dead. And then other men put flowers on them.'

'Men dead, put dead flowers.'

She wondered whether he had got it right. Perhaps she had better make it simpler. 'When men are dead other men put flowers on them. Men dead, men put flowers.'

'Men dead, flowers. Flowers, men dead.' He stood gazing around the room, assimilating the idea. Then his glance fell on the regiment of soldiers heaped up against the wall in the corner by the fireplace. 'Flowers, men dead. Men dead, flowers.'

Suddenly he darted to the corner and clutched an armful of the soldiers, many of whom were by this time missing an arm or leg, and laid them flat in a row on the hearthrug. Before Virginia could stop him he had grabbed the flower bowl from the sill and was balancing a peony head, broken off short, on each leaden chest. 'King-Alfred dead, Canute dead, Henry-Second dead.'

Canute's peony had fallen off. Appius rammed it back, head downwards. It stuck this time.

'King-John dead, Swalter-Raleigh dead, Philip-Sidney dead.'

He paused. There was still one soldier without a peony. 'Naplon dead.' He poised the flower triumphantly and then stood up. 'Dead.' He reviewed the line. 'Appius not dead.

Appius one great man. One great, great man.'

Virginia got up, amused, and began to collect the broken peonies. 'What a bad boy he is. Now all the poor flowers will die. Isn't Appius sorry?'

'Sorry?'

'Sorry the flowers will die. Appius doesn't like the pretty flowers to die, does he?'

'Appius like flowers?' He stared blankly. It had not occurred to him to consider whether he liked them or not.

Virginia put the depleted bowl back on the sill.

'Now mama is going to get tea. Appius can stay here and play or read to himself. There are plenty of nice books here besides lesson books.' She waved her hand towards the bottom shelf.

She went out.

'Appius read.' Passing by the row of prostrate soldiers, he gave the end one a kick which sent the file into an ignominious jumble of varnished limbs and helmets. 'Appius read. Appius more great man.'

He ran his hand along the bottom shelf, scratching at a binding here and there and leaving a book tipped outwards. Near the end of the row he came upon a large, flat volume, taller than the others.

That would do. Big man read big book. He gave it a tug and it fell out on to its face. Squatting on the floor, he opened it. Big picture. Horse, black and yellow. Big letter up above it. Z. Reading underneath: z-e-b-r-a. He spelt it out.

'Appius read one page.'

Over. The page wouldn't turn. Other way. The page turned; several pages. R. Rat. He knew that. The cat caught the rat.

'Appius read two pages.'

Book not right. Page not right. He knew it ought to turn

the other way. What was the matter with it? He shuffled it about on the floor, turning it all ways. Ah. That was right. The Animal Alphabet. Satisfied, he settled himself squarely.

First page. The Animal Alphabet again. No picture. Next page. Man, with no clothes on. Man, two-legged animal. Reading underneath: A-p-e.

A-p-e. What was that? He picked up the book and looked hard at it. A-p-e. That wasn't 'man.' What was it? He connected the letters slowly: A-p-e. What did that remind him of? He frowned.

Ape, ape, ape, ape, ape. Quick and short like that, it was. Boys! Ape, ape, ape. Like that, at him, Appius!

He sprang up, muttering, while the book fell from his knees and slid into the corner.

Ape!

He walked once or twice round the room, his eyes shifting quickly from side to side. 'Ape, ape, ape,' he muttered uneasily.

That was it. Wall. Boys. Bad boys. Bad boys say ape. Bad book call man ape.

Abruptly he stopped. He spoke slowly, remembering: 'Ape animal. Ape bad animal.' He walked up the room and back again, then his frown cleared.

'Not picture man; picture ape. Picture ape animal. See what, ape animal.'

He pulled the book out of its corner and tore at the leaves until he had found the picture again. A-p-e. There it was. But it was man. He knew it was man. He had seen a picture of man just like that, but he couldn't remember where. Was it Canute, or Henry-Second, or Philip-Sidney? He didn't know. Only this man had no clothes on. Why? And the book called man ape.

'Book bad!' He dashed it to the floor.

'Bad book say man ape. Book bad. Man great. Appius man.'

He wondered again, obscurely, inarticulately, what it was in this word 'ape' which stirred such anger within him. It had an enraging sound which dug into his mind like a chisel into soft wood, a little further at every tap, bruising, compressing, driving back the mind into itself at each repetition. He had never heard the word 'insult,' but in the darkness of his brain he knew that some part of himself was profoundly outraged by this barking cry; it smeared his soul with a slimy desecration, as if, sinking to rest among the ferns in the depths of his secret refuge, he had found the soft mud crawling with half-formed reptiles.

He shuddered at things felt rather than thought.

Years ago he had known this feeling, less distinctly, more childishly, when the insult had been levelled solely at himself; when the boys had shouted at him from the wall. Then he was a child, and his child's dignity had been wounded for a time. But this wound was far deeper because far more comprehensive. For was he not man? He had recognised his kinship with great men; the superiority, even, which he had over them; and now the whole dignity of man was threatened. A slur was cast not upon him alone but upon those who shared with him the kingship of the earth. They were wounded in him and he in them.

He sat there on the floor, the book crushed face downwards at his feet, and felt obscurely and half consciously as huge images loomed upwards into his brain and sank heavily, leaving black, gaping vacancies. His jaw was thrust slightly forward and his heavy under-lip drooped, showing the line of his teeth. His heavy eyelids blinked slowly up and down. His eyes were more puzzled than angry, and a little frightened.

'Appius. Tea's ready.'

Mama was calling him. He climbed on to his feet and picked up the book, looking furtively around him.

'Where? Mama not see.'

Some instinct which he did not question urged him to hide the book, to bury the insult where it could not touch him. 'Mama not know.'

'Appius, come along. Tea's in the dining-room. What are you doing?'

Mama was getting cross.

'Book go. Bad book go.' He thrust it down behind the books on the bottom shelf and crammed in a projecting piece of cover. It was out of sight. 'Book gone.'

His face cleared. He opened the door. 'Appius come,' he called, and clattered downstairs.

Virginia looked up in surprise as he came in. 'How long you were, darling. What was Appius doing?'

Usually he was in such a hurry for his meals. He sat down and mumbled sulkily: 'Appius play.'

'Well, he'll better have his tea quickly and get out into the garden. It's a beautiful evening.'

He needed some exercise, evidently. He was looking quite sulky and fretful. Perhaps she'd made him work too hard at his lessons. Still, he'd had half an hour's play just now.

Appius munched sullenly. Not want tea. Bad book. He had killed the bad book, though. 'Book gone,' he mumbled into his cup.

'What, darling?' But he didn't answer. 'Don't speak while you drink, dear. I've told you before.'

He gulped down the milky tea and bit into his bread. Not say mama. Book gone. Mama not know. He chewed. *Had* the book gone? He must see. He chewed more quickly.

How glum he was to-day. He'd certainly been indoors too

151

long. What he wanted was to get out and dig for a bit.

When he had finished she said: 'Now Appius can come out in the garden. Mama will sit on the verandah and Appius can dig. He'll like that, won't he?'

'Appius want play nursery.'

'Want to play in the nursery? But you've been in all the afternoon! Come in the garden with mama, there's a good boy, and then you can play in the nursery for a bit before bedtime. Come along. Mama is going to sit out here and watch you.' She went through on to the verandah and dragged her chair into the sun.

'Want play nursery.'

How determined he was. He wasn't often so stubborn as this. Well, it was better not to force him. She shrugged her shoulders.

'Very well. If you must, you must. Mama is going to stay here, and when you've had enough of the nursery you can come down, but you'd better come before all the sun goes.'

She sat down and took some knitting from the bag on her arm. Appius had gone already. What new craze was this for playing indoors? He'd soon get tired of it when he found she didn't come.

Chapter Nineteen

With his shoulder Appius pushed to the nursery door so that it banged. He stood glaring at the room from under lowered brows. His mouth was working. Book. Book gone? See.

He rummaged behind the row of picture books, his fingers scraping their shiny cardboard edges.

'Book here. Not gone.'

It came, wrenched upwards, tilting forwards, as it came, part of the row which had hidden it. 'Bad book.'

Flung down, it made a flat, resentful thud on the carpet. He crouched, and shuffled its pages until the picture of man, great man, lay facing him: man hideously libelled by three black, bold letters beneath his feet.

'Bad.'

He put his face down closer to it, scowling. He wriggled his feet out across the carpet behind him and lay with his mouth almost leaning upon the picture, studying it minutely.

No. There was no mistake. It was man. He knew that face: the proud, forward thrust of the jaw, the wide mouth slitting it, the eyes retreating into the shadow of the forehead, the little ears just showing around the corner. That was man's picture. It was not dog or horse or goat. It was man. He had seen this very picture before. It was Naplon, only here he had no clothes on.

Indignation seized him afresh. He flung the book hard against the fender and kicked it away as it rebounded at his feet.

'Naplon great man. Bad book say ape.' He ran up and down the room, gnawing the words in helpless anger. 'Bad. Naplon great man. Bad, bad book. Kill book fire.' He stopped short, faced by shiny, black, useless coal.

No fire. Summer. Mama in garden. Want Appius play garden. Mama. Mama kill bad book. He picked it up and lunged towards the door.

He stopped and opened his hand slowly so that the book fell.

'Not say mama.'

He stood still and his brow wrinkled. He rubbed his eyes with the back of his hand.

'Not say mama. Book bad.' He wavered. 'Naplon. Find Naplon.'

He turned to the bookcase, searching with his hands. Blue. Second Lessons in History. 'Naplon, great man.'

He turned the pages until Napoleon faced him, arms folded and brow lowered. He stroked the picture with pride, almost with affection. 'Naplon. Great man, Naplon. Bad book say ape.' His eyes clouded.

Napoleon seemed not to hear him, but he was frowning already. He had known what the book was saying before Appius found it out.

'Naplon see bad book.' Appius crouched again before the

alphabet and confronted Napoleon with the ape. 'Bad book say Naplon ape.'

Then he stopped suddenly, frowning again, a puzzled frown. Not Naplon. Picture man not Naplon. Man more big. Face more big. Not Naplon. What?

He dropped the Second Lessons in History and shuffled the alphabet pages in bewilderment. Man not Naplon. Naplon great man. Book say man ape. Not Naplon. He shuffled the leaves backwards and forwards, muttering all the time.

M-a-n. Man! The word had jumped at him from between the pages and jumped in again. It was there somewhere. He snatched the pages apart, wildly searching.

'Appius! Aren't you coming out? It will be too late soon. Come along at once.'

Mama calling.

'Mama not see.' He thrust the alphabet into the bookcase, then grabbed it out again. 'Book say man. Appius see.'

He listened, blinking rapidly.

'Appius come!' he bellowed, and waited again.

'Very well. Hurry up.'

He heard her go out and the chair scrape on the verandah tiles. Mama not come.

The pages shuffled over and over. There. In the middle. Man.

He lay down and nosed over the picture, under the letter M, of primitive man, with leopard skin thrown over one shoulder, leaning upon a club.

Man. Ape. Naplon. He drew back, blinking furiously. Man why? Ape why? Bad book say ape. Say man ape. Not say man ape. Say one man ape. Not say two man ape.

He turned back to the first page. Man. Appius see picture man. He waited, trying to remember. See picture man. This man. He turned back again. M-a-n. Man. This man not man. Face small. Arms white, neck white. No hair. Not man. M-a-n. Man?

'Why? Man. Ape. Why?'

He puzzled, desperately thinking. Ape animal. Perhaps that was the clue. Mama say ape animal. Bad boys say ape man. Then this was ape animal. He examined it again. But it was man.

'Appius *see* picture man. Man.' He slapped it with his palm. He turned to the other. Not man. Yet m-a-n spelt man.

'*Man*? Not?' He wavered backwards and forwards.

'Appius, come at once.' Mama was angry.

'Appius come,' he shouted. He crammed the alphabet into its hiding-place and scrambled downstairs.

Mama was angry. She was standing in the doorway, tapping her foot on the sill.

'That's twice I've had to call you. What were you doing? Well, can't you answer?'

He was shuffling from one foot to the other, staring past her out into the garden. Annoyed, she turned back to her chair.

'Well, you'd better get along now. You needn't think you'll mope in the nursery without any air until bedtime. There's the spade.' She pointed to where it lay on the ground. 'Get along and dig for half an hour and don't let me catch you sneaking back into the house.'

She took up her knitting and dug her needle into the first stitch of a row, drawing the wool very tight. She had dismissed him.

He stared at her resentfully for a minute and then went, grumbling, down the path towards the spade.

'Man digs the earth,' he muttered apathetically, prodding the soil. The formula had long ago become mechanical, part

156

of the ritual of existence like his prayers, spoken without significance or thought as a prelude to his labours, but to-day the words rang back at him as the flat of the spade clanged against a loose stone.

Man digs the earth. It echoed in his mind. Man. Appius man. Book say man ape. Picture man say ape. Why? Picture man what man? Picture man not Naplon. Canute? Henry-Second? He reviewed them in memory. Canute sit seashore. Henry-Second big beard, look at White Ship on sea. Not Canute, not Henry-Second. Man.

He dug fitfully, scratching the ground and flinging small showers of earth and stones into the air.

Man. Appius man. Appius? He hesitated, considered again, dug into the air: a big swing of the spade which stopped against something hard and then went through it with a cracking noise followed by a heavy flump on the ground. Rose tree killed. Mama see? He looked round anxiously. Yes, she had got up.

'Appius, what are you doing there?' Her voice was sharp, and her heels were coming tap-tap, quickly, along the path.

'Appius, how naughty you are.' She took him by the shoulder and shook him. 'Look what you've done. Tiresome child. You can't be trusted a moment.'

She snatched the spade out of his hand.

'Look at that. Look. You're completely stupid to-day. What's the matter with you? You ought to know better, a big boy like you.' She shook him hard, and her teeth clicked between the sentences. 'Come along in and go to bed at once. You ought to be ashamed of yourself. A big boy behaving like that.' She walked him smartly towards the house.

Boy. Big boy. The words jolted up and down as he was dragged over the gravel. Big boy Appius. Big boy. Picture big boy Appius. Picture! Appius big boy. Appius man. Picture man, Appius!

He spoke aloud in his excitement. 'Picture man, Appius. Appius see picture.'

He strained at Virginia's hand. She pulled him sharply to her side.

'What nonsense are you talking about a picture? No pictures for you to-night. You'll go straight to bed, and then perhaps you'll realise what a bad boy you are.'

She hauled him upstairs to the nursery.

Picture man, Appius. He repeated it in his mind almost joyfully, proud of having found the solution. He had forgotten that he had a picture, for he had not visited it for some weeks, not since the summer began. Picture of Appius in mama's room, and the picture in the book was the same.

Not Canute, not Naplon. Appius. Then he frowned. Book call Appius ape? Appius see.

As Virginia let go his hand to reach for his pyjamas he took a step towards the bookcase. Then he stopped. Mama not see. His eyes shifted to where she was hunting in the cupboard, her mouth set in a straight line. He shuffled back to the bedside and waited there sulkily until she brought the pyjamas and undressed him.

By the time she was downstairs he was out of bed again, shivering in the cool air from the open windows. He stuck his feet into the felt slippers which were standing near the foot of his bed, side by side as Virginia had slapped them down, and padded over to the bookcase.

He listened. Mama downstairs. Find bad book. Bad picture. Picture Appius? He clawed it out and settled on the carpet, taking care not to bump as he sat.

Picture Appius! Yes. He remembered now. Mama room,

Appius picture. Big boy Appius. That was what had reminded him. Appius grow great big man. He remembered that face, his face, the mouth and eyes and ears. Yes. This was his picture, only it had no clothes on. Rage leapt in him again, raced to his ears and made them tingle. Bad, bad, bad book. He grabbed at it, swung it at the full swing of his arm high above his head, then slowly lowered it again. Mama coming. He had heard her step in the hall. No. He listened, breathing quietly, turned ready to scuttle back to bed. Mama. Mama show Appius picture. Appius picture mama room. Appius want see picture. Mama.

She was still walking about the hall, locking the door into the garden, watering a plant on the central table. He could hear the chink of the tin watering-can as she set it down in its corner on the tiled floor.

Mama go. Appius want see.

While he waited, he ruffled the leaves of the book. It opened at the letter M where the page had been accordioned inwards by his bewildered fingers. He stared at it now. Man.

He had forgotten that. Picture man. Picture not Appius. He turned back to the beginning. Picture Appius. Back again. Picture man. His whole face was twisting in an effort to understand. Appius man. To and fro. Picture Appius. Picture man. Why?

Mama go dining-room. He heard the door shut behind her.

Mama go. Appius see picture. Appius see why. Clutching the crumpled book in one hand, he opened the door very softly and listened. Mama not come.

Appius picture mama room. He crept along the passage to her door, and pushed it. It was unlatched. He dropped the book on the bed and looked around.

Picture Appius. There it was, standing up against the

cupboard as he had seen it plenty of times before. Not very clear now, for the room was getting dark, but there was light enough for him to recognise it.

Picture Appius. He examined it with satisfaction, squaring his shoulders. Appius big man. He had almost forgotten the book.

Picture have pyjamas. He noticed this with wonder, then remembered. This was his picture and had to do what he did, not like the picture of Canute who always looked at the sea and wore the same crown day and night. That was because Canute was in a book.

Book. He remembered. Bad book.

As he picked it up it fell open at the picture of man. He examined it again, and frowned. He looked at his picture, and muttered. Not Appius. Book say man. Why? He rubbed his eyes, and looked from the picture to the mirror and back again, but he couldn't understand. A swift fog was rising in his brain as he tried to puzzle it out. His brain was feeling bluntly, now, as through a thick layer of cotton-wool. Man. Not man. Appius Not Appius. He turned back to the ape. Appius. No clothes. Book say ape.

Ape what?

Through the cotton-wool the tentacles of his brain had closed around something solid. Ape what? He scowled with the effort of memory. Bad boys say ape man. Ape what? Mama say ape animal.

Ape animal. Picture ape, picture ape-animal. Picture man, picture man.

His chest deflated after the effort. He put down the book and found himself looking into the eyes of picture-Appius.

Appius. Appius man. Picture-Appius, picture ape-animal. Why?

His brain began to grope again, but the fluffy layer had grown thicker. Appius. Picture-Appius. Great man. Book-picture ape-animal. He fumbled, clutching at the images by their blunt edges, finding no order in their muffled proximity. He frowned fiercely, scowling at mirror and book in turn. Book-picture Appius say ape-animal. Picture Appius, man. Man. Book-picture man, not Appius. He folded the book in two and held it against the mirror, beside his own face which grew larger the more closely he examined it.

Appius not man!

At last the brain tentacles had closed around a solid concept. Through a jagged gap in the wool they dragged it, sharp-edged, clear-cut, unquestionable, and dropped it with a dull thud into the soft, yielding mass of his consciousness. The idea stuck like a pointed stone hurled against flesh. It almost stunned him by the suddenness of its impact numbing him to its further implications. He stood with his mouth open, gaping at himself.

Appius not man. Slowly his hand fell open and the book slid down the polished surface of the mirror to his feet. His eyes glared uncomprehendingly at their own wonder; his feet shuffled, and met the fallen book. Book. Man. Appius not man. He crouched, and shuffled the book open again. Not man. What? The numbness was wearing off as the jagged stone edges sawed the raw surface of his consciousness.

What?

Doubt, scarcely comprehended, unexpressed, began to gnaw at him. Feverishly he searched for the other picture, crouching low before the mirror in the darkening room. His picture had crouched too, and glared at him when he looked up, showing its teeth in a wide, voiceless snarl.

Ape-animal. Appius. No clothes. Appius!

His throat was swelling. A rumbling far down in him was swiftly rising, rushing upwards to his mouth. His brain heard it and trembled. It was gripping his tongue, stiffening it, strangling words.

Appius. No clothes. 'Ape-animal!'

The words broke through in a shout. He hurled the book on to the floor and kicked it furiously. He tore off his pyjama coat and flung it across the room. It struck the dressing-table, and in its fall dragged brushes and pin-tray to clang against the boards. The lace cover hung, half off, and flapped in the wind. Appius kicked his slippers into the empty grate. His pyjama trousers caught, and lay sprawling across Virginia's bed. He flung up his arms and hurled himself against the mirror.

'Appius. *Ape!*'

The words were violently projected from his jaw, then overtaken and drowned by the howl which filled his swollen throat and burst upwards and outwards. It flooded his brain. There remained no images, no words, no wool even: nothing but darkness and howl, and red flares streaking the darkness. The whole of his short, powerful body crashed against the mirror; its fists beat and beat the shivered glass above its head.

Chapter Twenty

Had he heard her?

Virginia closed the door very softly and leant against the wall, outside in the passage, listening.

Surely he would hear the door-knob rattling, her hand was shaking so. But she mustn't let go, or he might come out. She ought to go in and be stern and make him get back to bed. She ought to call him firmly and face him without flinching and dominate him by her calm authority as she had always done. Only her legs were trembling so much that she mightn't be able to look firm in front of him. Supposing she hesitated or stammered. Besides, it was no good pretending to be firm. She must be firm. It was her mind, her unshaken will, that he obeyed.

He ought to put his pyjamas on, he'd get cold like that.

Was her voice steady enough? She whispered shakily, 'Appius.' She listened, holding her breath. Suppose he had heard her.

How had he got into her room? Why? What had happened to make him think about apes to-night? He must suddenly have become suspicious and gone to look at himself in the mirror to make sure. But why? She had left him in bed. What could have happened? He might have had some kind of warning dream, perhaps. But there hadn't been time for that.

He had been tiresome all day, but why this? Never mind that. He must be stopped. Somehow he had broken the mirror, of course, and she could hear the glass falling in splinters. He would cut himself.

What could she do? She was trembling less now. Perhaps she could go in. But if once she went in she wouldn't be able to come out again; she'd have to go on until he was quiet.

She stiffened herself against the wall, feeling her back and legs grow taut. A cord was tightly drawn through each. Could her knees bend, she wondered? She stood upright and listened again, the door-handle already turned. He seemed to be a little quieter now. His movements were slower; he must be getting tired. The roar had died down to a rumble in his throat. But she must be prepared.

She opened the door part way and stood looking at him without going in.

He was little more than a shadow in the dusk of the room: a short black shape, heavy and violent, moving with blurred outline against a grey rectangle of window. She could see that he had thrown off all his clothes; fur was standing out in a jagged ridge along his spine and in clotted tufts on his thighs and shoulders and hammering arms. She could not see his face.

She shivered and quickly switched on the light.

'Appius.'

That was done. It was firm, too. She must go in now.

He had heard her. He turned round, his hands dropping to his sides, and took a step towards her. By a fierce effort of will she stood motionless.

'Appius. Pyjamas.' Without taking her eyes from him, she pointed to the sprawling trousers.

Appius stopped. He thrust his head forwards in a line with his chest and muttered at her, the quick, non-human mutter which she had not heard for years. His eyes were shifting over her, around her and back again. They seemed to be smaller than usual, and red.

'Appius, pyjamas.' No change in tone. Appius stopped muttering. His throat was still working but no sound came out. His lower jaw was pushed forwards and his teeth showed above it. He stared at her out of his small, red eyes.

In his dark brain slow things were darkly moving. Mama angry. Appius pyjamas. Appius.

'Appius ape!'

The darkness slit. There were words for his rage. 'Appius ape!' He lurched towards her, arms flung up, hands clutching.

'Appius.'

She swayed backwards, but her feet stood firm, her hands grasped the edge of the door and the doorpost. They would not let her go back, she thought. She had stiffened them with her will, and now they held her prisoner.

'Appius,' she repeated. Her voice seemed to be lower than usual, she thought, hearing it from a distance. She had never spoken so savagely to him, look at him with such iron determination, such inexorable, unyielding, irresistible command.

Appius stopped. All his teeth glared at her, but there was fear in his eyes. He backed, snarling; then he hurled himself sideways upon the mirror, clawing at the broken edges.

'Appius ape! Ape, ape, ape!' He shouted himself into a frenzy again, flinging pieces of glass in all directions. He kept

165

his back turned upon Virginia. He had shut her out. Mama not see.

She waited until his fury had worn itself down. Then she shut the door behind her and came further into the room. It seemed that he would not attack her. He was too much afraid, even now. 'Appius. Pyjamas.'

'Appius ape. Ape, ape, ape.' He was beating the wood of the wardrobe where the glass had been torn away. He would not look round. He had only one thought, but he still knew vaguely that mama must not be there. He would not see her.

'Ape, ape. Appius ape.' The words had little meaning for him by this time. They formed a cry as elemental, almost, as directly expressive as the roar which had torn him and hidden his words in darkness.

'Appius, ape.' It was a howl of rage, a cry of pain; pain as far removed from understanding of its cause as the sting of an arrow sent by an unseen hand. He had been wounded. He did not know why or how, nor what part of him the arrow had destroyed. Appius ape. It had left a gaping sore, and the sore stung, and the words eased the sting.

His picture on the cupboard door was in some way responsible. He had killed the picture. Only half of it remained: a half without a head. All the central part of the mirror, the head and shoulders of Appius, lay scattered in fragments about the room. He was picking now at the uncracked edges, but no more would come away. Still, it was killed. It couldn't look at him any more, and cry 'ape.' It had no mouth.

Mama was behind him. She was angry. Pyjamas. He must put them on. He glanced down at himself. 'Appius, ape!' He turned upon her, shouting it, but met her eye. Mama angry.

'Appius, put on your pyjamas at once.'

Mama more angry. She was holding out the pyjama trousers,

staring at him steadily.

'Appius ape.' He muttered it defiantly, avoiding her eye.

Slowly he pulled them on while she watched him. Then she fetched the coat from where it hung on the dressing-table.

'Appius ape.'

She pushed his arms into the sleeves. If only he would stop repeating that. It was getting on her nerves. She must put him to bed and then he would be all right.

'Bed.' She took him by the shoulder, feeling her arm still stiffened, and guided him out of the room and along the passage. 'Now bed, quickly.'

As the nursery door swung open in front of him Appius stopped.

'Appius ape,' he said, glowering. It was a challenge to whatever might be watching him return, waiting to deride him. But the room, under the white electric light, was quite still, with blank, black windows, and he felt mama's thin hand pressing into his shoulder.

'Appius ape.' It was little more than an assertion, and he let himself be pushed towards the bed

'Get in quickly.' Virginia loosed him and went to draw down the blinds.

When her back was turned he stood still, sucking his fingers, and stared at the bed in front of him.

There it was, with the top of the sheet still rumpled where he had crept: out of it an hour or so before. Then, he had been Appius-man; now he was Appius-ape. Ape-animal. Suddenly, muttering the words over in this familiar room, he was struck for the first time by their full significance.

Ape-animal. He knew now how he had been hurt, what had been taken from him. He, Appius, was no longer man. No longer had he kinship with Canute and Naplon and Henry-

Second; no longer was he great man. He was not even man. Henry-Second and Canute and Naplon were no more his fellows; he was not greater but less than they. He was not man, but animal.

'Appius not man. Appius ape-animal!' He howled it at the room. Virginia, her hand still on the blind, trembled a little.

Appius was crouching on the bed, glaring with eyes which had almost disappeared under his brows. Ape-animal. What had dared to say so? Book. Bad book. And there it was. Book, books, hanging half out of the shelves as he had left them, some tumbled on the floor. He sprang from the bed, and in one bound was upon them, tearing them from their rows, hurling them at the walls and ceiling.

'Appius, stop. Do you hear?' Virginia was gripping his arm, bending over him and staring into his eyes, her face almost level with his. 'Stop that at once. Go to bed.'

He drew back as far as he could and turned his face away.

'Appius ape-animal.'

Virginia sighed quickly.

'Nonsense. Appius man. Go to bed.'

He strained his arm away from her hand and backed against the wall, in the corner beside the fireplace.

'Appius ape, Appius ape, Appius ape, ape, ape.' He barked it at her.

'Stop!' she almost screamed.

This was terrible. She couldn't go on like this. He was too much for her. Was he going mad? There was no end to this horrible cry. It went on and on, smashing like a hammer. It would never stop. It never varied. She was exhausted. He seemed as much awake as if it were midday, while she felt hollow with weariness. She supported herself against the bookcase and braced herself for a last effort. 'Appius man, I tell you. Appius *not* ape. Appius man. Now go to bed.'

'Appius ape,' he said. Then his foot struck against something. Canute.

There were the lead soldiers. Now surely he wouldn't start playing with them at this time of night. He must be quiet.

'Quick,' she urged. 'Bed.'

'Canute, Naplon, Henry-Second.'

He had got them all out in a row up against the wall. Well, at least they seemed to be diverting his attention from apes for a moment. He was looking at them almost kindly.

'Canute great man.'

But no, he was remembering.

'Man!'

He had seized Canute by the legs and was smashing him against Napoleon, and Napoleon against Henry the Second. He would break them all to pieces.

'Ape, ape!'

All three were crashed and bashed together; in a few moments the whole regiment was nothing but a heap of leaden heads and limbs.

'Appius ape!'

'Appius *man*, I tell you.' Virginia had seized him by both arms and was violently shaking him. 'Appius man. Man, man, man.'

She stopped suddenly and almost fell forwards on top of him. Was she going mad too? Well, this time he should go to bed. She gave him another shake and dragged him on to his feet.

'Bed at once, or mama will smash you as you've smashed the soldiers.'

She pushed him across the room, hands on his shoulders, shaking him as she went. At the bedside she held the clothes apart whilst he climbed in, then tucked them firmly around his neck.

'Sleep,' she hissed. 'And don't let me hear any more of you to-night.'

She had hardly turned away before both his hands had struggled up between his neck and the tightly drawn sheet. He stuffed them into his mouth. They hurt.

Out of the corner of her eye Virginia caught the movement. She turned back irritably. 'Now what's the matter with your hands? Take them out of your mouth at once and keep still.'

He took no notice, only looked at her thoughtfully across the shaggy wrists protruding from the pink gap of mouth. She thought: Of course, he must have cut himself with the glass. How very tiresome.

'Let mama see, then.'

She drew the hands out and examined them, struggling for patience. Yes. Several of the fingertips were slightly cut, oozing a drop or two of purplish blood. Clean cuts. Nothing serious. Sighing wearily, she dug into the cupboard for lint and disinfectant, and firmly bound the wriggling claws in pieces of linen.

'There. Now be a good boy and go to sleep.' She patted his head not ungently and again tucked in the clothes. Then she sank into the armchair beside the fireless grate and waited. The fire was laid, but she was too tired to put a match to it. She would only stay for a bit and see that Appius didn't get out of bed. When he had once got to sleep she could go.

She ought to think, too. There was a lot to be decided. What had happened to him to make him like this? No. That didn't matter so much. But what was she to do with him now? He'd got this idea into his head, heaven knew how, of being an ape. How could she get him out of it?

He just went on repeating it. If only he wouldn't be so obstinate she might be able to find out what was the matter with him and put it right. But he was always like that. It was only by accident that she ever found out what had set him off on an idea. She'd have no end of trouble rooting out the source of this ape business.

That didn't matter, though. How could she make him see that it was all nonsense? That was what she must consider. How could she convince him and make him forget about it?

Oh, she didn't know. She was so tired. Much too tired to think it out. Why did he make such problems? She couldn't decide anything to-night. She was worn out. She seemed to be melted into the chair, and yet its pressure was weighing upon her. If only she could go right through, sink into air, touch no solid body at all.

Tell him something about evolution. What was it? She couldn't remember. Something about brain rapidly evolving; change not apparent. Must be grateful. Child's obligation to parent. Man's brain rapidly evolved. No time to change form. Must be grateful.

She drifted, half dozing, her eyes open, her arms laid lifeless along the arms of the chair.

Chapter Twenty-One

Appius lay in bed and thought: Appius ape. Apeanimal Appius.

He tossed to and fro, wide awake, but he dared not get out of bed again because mama was very angry, angrier than she had ever been. Mama more, more angry. Why? Appius ape. Mama angry Appius ape-animal.

Ape. In the stillness of the room the word hummed about him, stinging his flesh. He writhed, speared upon it, the prick gnawing deeper as he tossed.

Ape. The room blared it at him. The scattered books, the empty shelves, the desk, the rug, the grate, even the heap of lead which once had been great men: all the things he had ruled because he was man reviled him now. His kingdom mocked him. The electric bulb in the ceiling was a cold, unblinking eye staring down full upon his shame. Darkness was dead. It would not hide him any more. Even down under the bedclothes the light followed him. He screwed up his eyes as tight as they would go, but the light danced and gibed under his lids. Ape, ape, ape-animal.

Nowhere to hide. No escape. Animal, not man. The world was not his. He was alone. He was mocked. Ape, ape, look at the ape. Look at the ape wi' trowsis orn. Alone, mocked, betrayed.

Back to the tunnel. Down into sleep. Down, far down, into himself. Down through the quiet, dark tunnel into the moist, yielding mould where the great leaves swept over him, where insects hummed distantly, far above in the protecting fern.

There was no tunnel. There were no leaves. There was no darkness. It was gone. He closed his eyes; the light hissed. He opened them; it blared. Ape, ape, ape. His refuge was gone. He himself was gone. His world had rejected him, scoffed him back into the world of men where the light would gibe at him for ever. Ape, ape, ape. Ape-animal.

He tossed in agony. Why? Why? Why cast out? Why scorned? Why animal? Ape. Ape-animal.

The light beat relentlessly; its eye was expressionless. Not man. Why? No tunnel. Why? Appius ape. Why?

In torment he tossed himself upright in the bed. He sat staring around for deliverance in the quiet, lighted room.

Mama. There was mama sitting very still in the chair, looking straight in front of her, not seeing Appius. Mama, mama had said Appius was man. Then why was Appius ape? Why? He fell out of bed and shuffled over to her, forgetting in his urgency all fear of her anger.

'Mama!' It was a cry for help. 'Mama. Appius ape. Why?'

She started.

'Appius? What is it? What's the matter?' She was trembling, partly with cold, partly with the shock of awakening. She had been dozing uneasily while her tired brain groped relentlessly along the tortuous windings of unreason, dimly conscious of, but unpitying, her body's cramp and chill. She dragged herself

173

upright in the chair and forced her eyes to focus Appius as he faced her in his pyjamas, and her brain to register the meaning of his words.

'What's the matter?' Her tongue felt stiff and spoke with difficulty, but her brain was clearing a little. 'Go back to bed at once. You'll get cold standing about with no slippers or dressing-gown.'

He seemed not to hear her.

'Mama. Appius ape. Why? Mama say Appius man. Why? Appius ape. Why?'

She stared at him, trying to grasp the sense of his words. Ape. Man. Couldn't he leave that tangle alone for to-night? All the evening; and now, when she'd actually got him to sleep, he must wake and start it again.

'Come here.' She caught him by the wrist and drew him nearer. 'Now listen to me.' Summoning all her wandering attention, she focused it upon him.

'I tell you Appius is man. Man, man, man. Will that do? Appius *man*. Now go to bed and don't think about it any more.' She dropped his wrist and pointed to the bed. 'Run along, there's a good boy. Mama is tired.'

Appius let his hand fall where she had dropped it, on the arm of her chair. He took no notice of her pointing finger, but stared at her face, frowning. Bewilderment and his need to understand made him disregard her order.

'Appius want find.' He paused, striving to express his problem, to make her understand the urgency of his need for enlightenment. 'Appius want find. Appius ape. Mama say Appius man. Why?'

Hopefully he watched her mouth. Mama would explain if only he could make her see what he wanted. He did not for a moment doubt that she knew. Mama unknowing would be a contradiction in terms. Mama always knew. When she did not tell him something it was because she was angry. If she were not angry now she would explain away this tangle of ape-animal-man. She was mama.

It had never occurred to him to include her in any category. Among the ruins of his world she alone had remained firm, uninvolved and unquestioned. Mama was above and distinct from man and ape equally, partaking of the nature of neither, understanding both, uninterested in and scorning their rivalry. But she would explain. Whilst ape and man might struggle for possession of the world, mama would stand aloof holding it out of reach, watching with calm eyes, her finger ready to point out bed to the vanquished.

'Appius ape. Mama say Appius man. Mama say why.'

But mama was angry. Suddenly she was sitting up straighter than ever, on the edge of the chair, and frowning at him, her eyes bright and pointed.

'Appius, I'm surprised at you. I'm surprised that you should question my wisdom or the way I have brought you up. Is this your gratitude? It's a pity you don't know what a life I've saved you from.'

She spoke bitterly, hearing her own words, straining from their inadequacy a sharper bitterness. How stilted, she thought as their echo reached her; how unconvincing, how cold. Yet, heaven knew, she felt deeply enough about this. Her brain was exhausted, was refusing its task of expression. She sat silent, gripping the chair-arms, staring not at Appius but past him at the carpet a long way off and the litter in front of the book shelves. All the books he had thrown about.

So he knew, she thought. Somehow he had found out, and now he was accusing her of having deceived him, brought him up to believe himself man, and put him at the mercy of this or some other disillusionment. What else could he mean? She had wondered whether she should tell him. Well, he had found out now for himself and this was how he took it.

She smiled crookedly, remembering how she had planned to tell him one day when he was grown up; had imagined how he would thank her and how absorbed he would be in tracing with her the long course of his unique development. She had known how he would look at her with wonder, finding that here, in this simple mama he had known all his life, was a creative artist, the god who had moulded him out of clay. That was to have been when the experiment was completed.

But, after all, wasn't it completed? Here he was, questioning her conduct, asking for explanations. It was upsetting, but all the same it proved that she had succeeded, made him capable of examining his own condition, made him self-conscious. Wasn't this indeed the test of humanity, the distinguishing mark of man: a capacity for self-consciousness?

And this was how he took it, she reflected again. There he was, standing glowering at her, not realising at all how much he owed her, incapable of appreciating how great a gift she had made him.

'Well, what's the matter?' Disappointment had sharpened her voice. 'Aren't you satisfied with what you are? Don't you like being a man? Would you rather be sent back to the jungle and live in a tree? I'm afraid you'd soon fall out of it, Appius. You weren't so good at climbing the last time you tried. And you might find it uncomfortable walking about without shoes or clothes.'

She stopped, caught suddenly by the thought: that's true. He couldn't live in the jungle now. He couldn't live except under human conditions. And yet...

Nonsense. She drew her lips into a tighter line. He's a man.

What does he want with the jungle now? Jungle, indeed. Is that all he gives for his humanity? She looked at him a trifle contemptuously, waiting.

'Appius why? Mama say.' Appius stammered. Mama was angry. He couldn't make her tell him. She only talked a lot of things he didn't understand. But he stuck to his point: 'Appius ape. Mama say Appius man. Why?'

'Listen to me.'

She leant back and drew him on to her knee, fighting for patience. She would have to explain it all to him, she supposed. But how tiresome it was, just when she was so tired. Why couldn't he be sensible?

'Now listen.' She drew a deep breath. Appius was watching her intently. At last mama was going to tell him. 'Long ago, when the world began, there were no men. Only apes.'

That was a good beginning.

'Now you know what apes are like.'

'Appius ape. Why? Mama say Appius man.'

'Be quiet.' She frowned. What had she been saying? Oh, yes. 'Only apes. Now apes are animals.'

'Ape-animal Appius. Why?'

'*Will* you be quiet?' She shook him irritably, trying to collect her thoughts again. Really he was too tiresome.

'I've told you there were no men.' She was plunging desperately. 'Now that's to say, there were no men as they are now. They were apes. Not exactly apes, but men like apes, with no brains.'

Brains. That was the clue.

'They had no brains. They lived in trees and ate leaves and walked on all-fours, not on two legs like man. That's to say, as men do now. Now'—she frowned, clinging to the thread of her thought—'now. Apes now behave as men did then. That's

177

to say, these creatures who weren't exactly men and weren't, exactly apes. Now I've said they lived in the jungle. You know what the jungle is like; it's a huge forest full of trees, and then men, who were really apes, lived in them and swung from tree to tree. Now one day...'

She stopped, aghast. What had she meant to say next? What was this leading up to?

She repeated, thinking desperately: 'They lived in the jungle. The whole world was jungle then.'

Her mind swept backwards and forwards over the phrases, but she couldn't remember what should follow. Yet she knew that the whole argument was there in her mind, and a good argument, too: a clear rapid survey of evolution, leading up to—what? It cleared up all the problems of the situation. But it had gone. Her last words only remained on her lips, washed up by a tide of meaning which had receded and left them stranded there. If only she could remember the main point: how the explanation fitted on to the account of evolution.

But she must say something quickly. Appius was watching her. He was opening his mouth to ask his hideous question. She tried to give herself confidence with a brisk beginning. 'Well, now. Long ago these creatures who were neither man nor ape lived in the jungle.' She had caught it again; saw it unrolling in front of her, a long shining thread. 'They lived in trees in the jungle which was all over the world. And then one day, one day...'

Her voice trailed off into silence. No more. Her tired brain refused the jump. The taut thread had been cut under her hand; she could glimpse it streaking away into the distance, out of sight in a moment, like an express train from a slipped carriage. Only a fragment remained, speeding for a moment with parasitical force, but rapidly slowing up, coming to a dead stop.

Appius slipped his problem into the pause. 'Appius ape. Mama say Appius man. Why?'

'But don't you see?' Her voice was rising unsteadily. 'I'm trying to explain to you. Don't be so tiresome.'

Why couldn't he see? It wasn't fair, when she was so tired.

'Mama say Appius man. Why?'

'Oh, stop. Can't you stop?'

Suddenly she let her head drop on to the arm of the chair and cried hysterically. Appius slid from her knee and stood looking at her in amazement. Mama was making queer noises, different from any he had heard before, noises that meant nothing. She was doubled up in a queer way, too, and her shoulders were rocking about, sometimes from side to side and sometimes up and down. Her face was hidden. He had never noticed much of mama apart from her face. It was that which had praised or scolded, ordered or allowed. This heaving back of lilac wool, this tousled head with bits of hair straggling down and clinging to the wool, were unfamiliar to him. And the noises frightened him. Without taking his eyes from Virginia, he crept backwards to the far end of the hearthrug and sat there, up against the bookcase, watching her.

She was talking again now, but without lifting her head; talking in a strange husky voice muffled in the small space between her arms and the arm of the chair. She made little gasping noises between the sentences.

'Appius,' she was saying, 'you don't understand, or you wouldn't speak to me like this. You mustn't. You don't know. I was so lonely. I wanted you to grow up as my child. I wanted you to be human. I wanted you to be something even more than a child, something I'd made with my own brain out of

179

nothing, and shaped as I wanted it, and watched grow. Like having a plant and watering it every day and training it, and then seeing it grow into a great, spreading tree to give you shade and let you rest under it. I wanted you to be like that to me, Appius, because I was alone and knew I should still be alone when I was old. I wanted you to be like that tree, and let me lean upon you when I was old and you were grown up, so that I shouldn't be alone. I wanted to be clever, too, and show people that I could make you human, but I wanted the other most. Can't you understand?

'It's true. I didn't care about the experiment, really, after the first. I only wanted you to be human and talk to me. And I thought perhaps you'd grow to be fond of me, too, if I'd always looked after you when you were small. And I had to pretend you were my child so that the experiment would work; I mean, so that you'd grow up to be human as you did. And I did think, too, that you might be grateful when you knew what I'd done for you; only that doesn't matter. But don't reproach me, Appius darling. You do see I couldn't help deceiving you, don't you? And all the time I was thinking of your good, really, and how happy we should be together when you grew up and we could talk about it all. And now we can, can't we? Oh, don't spoil it all now. Don't blame me too much.'

She threw herself back, suddenly exhausted, and wiped her swollen face. What was Appius doing, she wondered? Why didn't he say something? Ah. There he was, sitting quietly on the rug, looking at her. What must he be thinking of her, breaking down like this? She hadn't meant to say so much, either. She dabbed at her eyes and tried to smile at him.

'Come along, darling. Say he isn't cross with mama.'

She held out her hand to him and was surprised to find that it was heavy. She dropped it on to her knee and closed her eyes wearily.

'Come, darling. You really must go to bed now. The night is nearly over.'

How strange that he didn't move. Then, looking more closely, she saw that he was dozing, his eyes nearly shut. He was keeping his balance only because his hands were on the rug, propping him. She laughed chokily.

'Poor little Appius. Has mama kept him up, then? Come along, we'll put him to bed.' She got up and went over to him, swaying as she walked, against the fender.

'Bed,' she said gently, tapping his shoulder. He would have to get up; she couldn't possibly lift him; when she tried to grip his arm her hand fell open nervelessly, refusing to hold. There was no strength left in her; she felt completely hollowed out. 'Bed, Appius,' she repeated shakily.

Without a word he raised his lids and dropped them again over eyes full of sleep. Then he stumbled across the room and crawled into bed. He was asleep again already.

Virginia dragged herself along the passage, leaning against the wall as she went. In her room the windows were still open and a cold dawn was creeping in, making the furniture large and grey.

She knew that the floor must be covered with broken glass; here and there a piece glinted in a chance ray of light. But she didn't care. Throwing herself on the bed, she drew the eiderdown over her and lay unconscious, half fainting, half asleep, until midday.

Chapter Twenty-Two

For some time Virginia tossed restlessly. The bedclothes must have fallen off; she was cold, especially in her feet. At the same time she felt strangely cramped and uncomfortable, as if her nightgown had got twisted up around her. Then she remembered: she had not undressed, and the eiderdown must have slipped. She struggled to open her eyes, but the daylight was pouring on to her lids, weighting them down, and they were gummy and stuck at the edges. She dragged them apart, the fraction of an inch. A blade of light slipped in through the chink and drew a fine slit across her brain. They closed again, and throbbed.

It was broad daylight. There was even sunlight in the room, she thought. It must be very late. She ought to see what Appius was doing. He had gone to bed as late as she had, though, and must still be sleeping.

She tossed again. Whatever had happened last night? He had worn her down completely, and then she had talked a lot about herself, telling him far more than she had meant to.

What had she said? She had been trying to show him how it

was that he might look like an ape though he was really a man, but she had been muddled, she supposed, in her explanation. And then he had accused her, hadn't he, of deceiving him about his origin? Or of cheating him of his own life? What was it? Anyway, it had been too much for her, just then.

How stupid. Why hadn't she kept calm and given him a quiet, clear, dignified explanation? She hadn't tackled that situation at all well. She didn't even know, now, how much he had grasped of what she had said, nor what he thought of her, nor whether he still thought he was an ape or not. What kind of mood would she find him in this morning? Well, she must get up and see. There'll be another situation to tackle, probably, and this time she must be efficient.

Again her lids struggled against the light. Then she rolled over on to her side farther from the window and, shading her eyes, examined the watch which was still strapped to her wrist. One o'clock, if it hadn't stopped. She listened, staring at the dial with the exaggerated care of a blurred mind. Then she slid her feet down on to the floor and slowly stood up, noticing that her throat was parched and her skin cold and damp, like the flesh of a dead chicken. She slipped off her clothes and got into dressing-gown and slippers, went across to the bathroom and washed. No time for a bath. It might have freshened her, but she must go quickly and see what Appius was doing.

What a state the room was in, she thought as she came back. A chill wind from the wide-open windows was flapping the curtains up and down. She unhooked one which had caught on the dressing-table mirror, shut the windows and straightened a picture which had been knocked out of place. There were pieces of glass everywhere, and most of the toilet things were on the floor. The wardrobe had its mirror ending in a jagged line half-way up and beginning again for an inch or so at the top where Appius had been unable to reach it. The bed, with counterpane rumpled and pleated, and eiderdown slipping off at one side, gave an air of dismal dissipation to the room. Virginia straightened the clothes and plumped up the pillow. That was better. The glass she'd have to sweep up later.

When she got to the nursery she found Appius lying in bed, blinking and pulling at the edge of the sheet.

'Appius want get up,' he said fretfully.

She pulled up the blinds, letting some pale sunshine into the room, and put a match to the fire, for it was a gusty day. In spite of her aching head and a vague feeling of sickness, she was cheered by the sight of Appius. He was sleepy and cross, but he seemed otherwise to have got over yesterday. Perhaps he had even forgotten about it.

'Appius want get up.'

'Yes, very well. He can get up quickly and have his bath.'

She washed and partly dressed him and left him to finish while she went downstairs to get a meal. Tea, she thought. It would do both of them good.

Appius struggled into his jersey and went over to the fire which was crackling, gathering strength. He stood looking down at it, frowning.

'Appius want. Appius want.'

He was puzzled. He didn't want to play, or to go out, or even to eat, and, yet he wasn't happy. His head was heavy, and tight inside, and has mouth was dry. He looked fretfully around to find out what it was he wanted and noticed the untidy bookcase with books strewn about the floor. A few were still leaning dejectedly against the ends of the shelves and here and there an odd one lay flat and isolated. They reminded him. 'Appius ape,' he said, sulkily and without emotion, as if repeating a lesson.

He told the fire, and his toe kicked at the fender with faint resentment, but not hard. It hurt his head to move suddenly or to think. Besides, it didn't matter. Appius want. What was it?

Then Virginia came back with the tray and set it on the table which she had drawn up to the fireplace. Appius stared sullenly at his bowl of bread and milk. He knew that the picture of Miss Muffet and the spider was at the bottom waiting for him to eat his way through, but he didn't want to find it to-day. He drank a little, first, from the cup of milky tea which stood beside the bowl.

'Appius ape,' he muttered into it.

Virginia looked up quickly. So that was it. He was still harping on that. Probably he hadn't heard, or understood, her explanation last night. She'd have to talk to him again presently, when she was more rested.

She sipped her tea. The hot liquid forced its way down the clenched passage of her throat, opening up as it went the frozen channels of sense. As she sipped, her eyes and brain ceased to throb, her ears to be stoppered with wooden blocks. Heat seemed to radiate through her, to be diverted like a river in flood along the dried-up veins until it reached outwards to the skin, thawing and making it supple. The dead flesh lived.

She glanced across the table and saw that Appius had settled down to the bread and milk and was munching conscientiously. What was he thinking about? She must find out for certain and tackle that ape problem if it still existed. Evidently it did.

'Well, darling,' she began brightly, 'how is Appius feeling after his long morning in bed?' Appius chewed. He was feeling more contented now that he had swallowed most of the bread and milk. He scooped up the last sop of bread from the head of Miss Muffet and scraped the bowl clean. Mama was speaking.

There was something he had to ask her, he remembered now. He looked up, waving his spoon so that some drops of milk were spattered on the cloth and into the fender beside him.

'Appius man. Appius ape. Why?' He waved the spoon again, glad that he had remembered.

That was it. There were two things, Appius man and Appius ape, and he couldn't get them straightened out. Mama must tell him. For the moment the implications of her verdict did not trouble him. Whether Appius man or Appius ape, Appius was having breakfast by the nursery fire. It was dancing cheerfully and warming him, and the bread and milk he had eaten had made him feel strong. But he wanted the muddle cleared up; he didn't like things he didn't understand. So he scowled a little at mama as he waved the spoon.

'Appius man. Appius ape. Why?' Then he remembered that ape was a bad animal, and scowled more fiercely. 'Appius man. Appius not ape. Why Appius ape?'

'Why, darling, of course Appius is man,' Virginia smiled at him, relieved. At least he wasn't going to reproach her as he had last night. He seemed to be more reasonable to-day. She would be able to make him understand. He seemed, too, to know in a way that he really wasn't an ape; only of course he couldn't be expected to take in her explanation all at once, poor little fellow. She got up and pushed the table back from the hearthrug without troubling to clear it.

'Appius come along and sit on mama's knee, and she'll tell him all about it.'

She sat back in the armchair and planted him firmly in the crook of her arm.

'Now listen.' She settled herself more comfortably. 'It's quite simple, really, only Appius must listen carefully or he won't understand.

'When the world began there were no men in it, only animals, all the animals Appius knows; and one of them was the ape.

'Now keep still.

'The world was all like a garden, a beautiful garden in which the animals played about together, and the ape among them.

'Now you know the story I told you, a long time ago, about Adam eating the apple and being turned out of the garden. Well, Appius is old enough now to know the real meaning of that story. The garden was the whole world before man came into it, and Adam was this ape we're talking about who was playing happily with all the other animals. You remember that Adam was turned out of the garden because he ate the apple from the tree of knowledge. Now that means that Adam, our ape, suddenly wanted to know. He became curious. We don't know why, but he did. His brain, which until then had done nothing but tell him when he was hungry or sleepy, now began to work. He began to think. And when he began to think he ceased to be an ape and became a man; a very primitive man, because he hadn't thought much yet, but still a man. You understand, darling? Ape became man when he began to think.'

Appius was staring at his knees and seemed to be listening attentively. She went on.

'Now when ape had begun to think and become man he wouldn't play any more with the other animals, he was too busy thinking. Besides, he wanted to rule the other animals instead of playing with them, because he was stronger than they were, now that he had a brain, and he saw that he could make them do what he wanted. So he tried to make them work for him. Some of the animals did as he told them, like the dog and horse, and some refused and fought him, like the lion, and some others simply were afraid and ran away whenever they saw him coming, like the rabbit.

'So now you see, the world was no longer a garden in which the animals played happily together, but a place where man was cross with them and they fought him and one another and were afraid.

'So the story tells us that when Adam had eaten the apple he was thrown out of the Garden of Eden and was never happy again; but what really happened was that the garden and the happiness which had been in it ceased to exist when the ape found a brain and became man. And man was unhappy afterwards as well as the other animals, not because God told him to be, but because the brain he had found made him unhappy. It would think, and make him worry about a lot of things which would never have troubled him at all if he'd been content to be like the other animals. It made him want clothes and wealth and power, so that he was unhappy if he hadn't got them. It even made him worry about what he ought to do, and even about whether he ought to be happy, and about what it was that made him different from the other animals and whose fault it was that he hadn't got all he wanted. And because he didn't know that it was his own brain which had done it and that he'd have been happy if only the brain hadn't come, he imagined a person called God who ruled him as he ruled the other animals. So he was afraid of this God and made up the story about him which I told you when you were a very little boy, because all little boys have to be told the story so that when they grow up they can see how foolish man was, and be wiser themselves. Because, you see, all man's unhappiness really comes out of his own brain, and he's got nobody to be afraid of at all.' Virginia paused, surprised at her own eloquence and the clarity of her brain.

She had never got all these ideas so straight before, she thought. Talking to Appius, trying to put things simply for him, had made her see what was evidently the truth, and so obvious, really. It had helped her to reconcile the unrelated and sometimes contradictory teachings which had slept side by side in her memory for many years: her father's lessons on Sunday afternoons; some university lectures on evolution; a smattering of text-book philosophy.

'I think, therefore I am.' How true that was, and how well it fitted in with the theory she had outlined. Had she, by chance, stumbled upon the simple, ultimate meaning of all the creation myths; accidentally found the reconciliation point of science and religion?

She was quite excited. She must try not to forget what she had just said; must write it down.

Then she remembered Appius. His attention had wandered to his hands and the finger bandages which by now were rather grubby, she noticed. But he turned and looked at her as she spoke to him.

'Now, darling, I expect you don't understand *all* that mama has been saying; you'll have to wait until you're a little older still. But what I want Appius to remember is this. First of all there were only apes. Then some of these apes found brains. Some didn't, we don't know why, but perhaps they lived in a different part of the garden and didn't meet the others; they just went on being apes and still are to-day. But those who grew brains became men, and, ever since, they've ruled the apes and all the other animals; so you see it's better to be a man even if his brain does make him unhappy at times. And the only difference between ape and man is that man has a brain and ape hasn't. You see?'

She was speaking slowly and carefully. 'Ape without brain is

189

an animal. Ape with brain is a man.'

Appius was puzzled. He had grasped that she was going to settle the problem which troubled him, so at first he had tried to listen. But then she had gone on talking instead of settling it, and he had found his fingers more interesting. He couldn't get the knots undone, but it was fun to pull at a bandage until it had made a corkscrew all the way down his finger instead of a little tight pad at the tip. But now he frowned to show that he was attending.

He's understood, she thought. He's thinking. She went on: 'Now for Appius.'

He sat up straighter.

'Appius was ape.'

'Appius man,' he muttered.

He doesn't like that, she thought. I must be careful.

'Appius was ape when he was very small. Then he grew a brain because mama helped him. So now he is man. Does Appius understand?'

'Appius ape. Appius man.' He frowned. She was only saying the same things over again.

She reduced it to its lowest terms. 'Appius small, ape. Appius big'—she laid a hand on his shoulder—'man.'

He considered. 'Appius small, ape. Appius big, man,' he repeated. He frowned.

After a moment his face cleared.

'Appius big.' He slipped from her lap and stood facing her. 'Appius man.' He slapped himself on the chest.

'That's right, darling. Appius man.'

'Man, man. Appius man.' He repeated it many times. He seemed to be trying to convince himself. 'Mama say Appius man.'

'Yes, darling.'

190

So he really was satisfied at last, was he?

'Appius man.' He muttered it to the fire and then to the window behind Virginia's chair. He couldn't reach her desk which was shut off in the corner, so he shouted to it. Then he went around the room, telling the next window, and the bed and the cupboard and the door, his voice gaining confidence each time. When he came round again to the bookshelves he kicked them disdainfully. Then he turned to Virginia. 'Appius man want play,' he commanded.

'Very well, run along into the garden. Mama will come presently. Here, you must have your coat, though.'

She caught him at the door, wrapped him up and watched him trot along the passage. He stopped at the bathroom door and put his head in. 'Appius man,' he told the bath. Then he ran downstairs.

From the window Virginia watched him wander on to the lawn, kicking up worm castings with his toes. Then she settled quickly at her writing-table and took a clean sheet of paper. 'Evolution Theory,' she headed it. 'Explanation Given to Appius.'

She wrote.

Chapter Twenty-Three

A week later Appius, slouching along one of the garden paths, struck his foot against something which was sticking out from under a low-growing barberry bush. 'Spade,' he said, surprised, when he had dragged it out.

He had not played with it for more than a week. On several days the weather had been bad enough for Virginia to keep him indoors. She was glad of the excuse to have him under her eye, for he had been strangely silent and listless ever since the question of his origin had been settled. When she let him go out he only strolled about the garden, kicking up pebbles, and now and then chasing a bird with a vicious pleasure she had not noticed in him before. He had been good enough in the house, and quiet, but not so cheerful as usual. He seemed to obey more from compulsion than from a wish to please her, she thought. But his sulkiness must come from the shock he had had. No doubt, too, he was thinking over for himself all she had told him. Watching him now from the dining-room window, she wished that he would dig as he used to; it would do him so much more good than mooning about like that.

But she hadn't suggested it. It was better to leave him alone to recover himself gradually.

Then she saw him stoop and pick up the spade. Splendid. If he had some good exercise he would be able to start lessons again. She turned back to the table she *was* clearing.

Appius picked up the spade and looked at it without interest. He had long ago despaired of finding the world which mama had told him was hidden under the garden. He had even forgotten, now, that it was there, waiting for him to find and rule it. It was merely out of habit that he set the spade in position and his foot ready to push.

'Man digs the earth.' The formula had been uttered before he realised that he was going to speak. He heard it, and frowned. It arrested him in the act of lifting his weight to drop it heavily downwards. His foot slid from the blade and he stood still, leaning with both hands on the handle.

'Man.' He frowned again. 'Man digs the earth. Appius man.' But his voice held little conviction. 'Appius man. Mama say Appius man.' He was trying to be sure. He *was* sure. Yet the book had said ape. He let go the spade and stood thinking, hands in pockets.

Book say ape. Mama say man. Why? But he had asked mama that, and she had said lots and lots. Her mouth had twisted and opened and shut and twisted again for longer than it ever had before, until he was tired of watching it. And he knew that she had been talking about that, because he had heard her say ape man ape, man ape man, over and over. Then she had said Appius man. So it was Appius man. But all the same the book had said Appius ape. He wriggled his head about, trying to decide.

Man, ape. He thought of them now with almost equal animosity. They bothered him alike, making him puzzle about them all the time, whether he were playing or eating, distracting his attention when mama was speaking to him so that he didn't hear and she was cross.

Man. Ape. He considered them. He disliked them both. Suddenly a solution came from somewhere outside his puzzled thoughts, avoided them, and plunged directly to his hands. The hands slid from his pockets. They seized the spade and hurled it as far as they could into the middle of a thick prickly barberry bush where he couldn't see it any more. 'Man go. Ape go,' he shouted. Then he turned and walked on down the path, thinking again.

At the bend in the path he stopped and raised his head. He addressed the wall in front of him, the pear trees, the lawn stretching out on his left hand. The garden was quiet, awaiting his announcement. 'Appius,' he said with intense conviction, and turned the corner.

Presently he heard mama calling him. 'Come along. Time for lessons.'

The exercise had done him good, she thought as he came up to her at the dining-room window. He was walking more briskly and looked altogether brighter than he had for some days. Now he'd better plunge straight into lessons again without her making any comment on the interruption. He must get back into his normal routine.

'Writing,' she said when they had reached the nursery. She settled him with a copy-book. Then she considered, leaning on her elbows, watching him from the far side of her desk.

It might not be wise to go back at once to history. There were too many references to great men, and although Appius had seemed to be satisfied with her explanations the sight of the familiar pages might upset him again. Geography, too, he had insisted upon associating exclusively with man. She would have to start him upon arithmetic soon, since a tutor was now out of the question for a time. Even with the greatest care in the selection of a candidate there might be an accident. With the best intentions in the world, a tutor, who after all had not had her experience of Appius, might upset him by some unguarded allusion. Untold harm could be done in a moment.

No, she would teach him herself, at least for several years to come, until he had quite outgrown his childish fancies and difficulties, and get him thoroughly grounded in all subjects. She must choose a simple arithmetic book.

But meanwhile she must teach him something to-day. He had finished his copy and was looking up, waiting for her to tell him what to do next. In a moment he would be thinking about history.

She looked desperately around and noticed on the window-sill the flower bowl which that morning she had filled with chrysanthemums.

She called him. 'Come here, darling, and look at the beautiful flowers mama has brought in.'

He came, and looked at them obediently, without interest.

'Flowers,' he said.

'Yes, dear. But they're not only flowers. They're beautiful. *Beautiful* flowers, aren't they?'

'Flowers,' he insisted.

'Yes, flowers.' She explained patiently: 'Appius doesn't know yet what "beautiful" means, but mama will tell him.'

She searched her mind for the simplest definition. 'Things are beautiful when looking at them gives us pleasure. Appius likes to look at the flowers, so the flowers are beautiful. '"Beautiful flowers," say that, darling.'

Appius was puzzled. They were flowers. All things that stood in bowls were flowers, and so were things which grew in the garden, when they weren't trees. But mama wanted him to say some more about them. What had she told him about flowers?

Now what is he frowning about, Virginia wondered.

Appius thought. Flowers. Flowers. People dead, people put flowers. That was it. But what was dead? Not mama. Not Appius. Flowers on window-sill.

'Now, darling, come along.'

Mama was getting impatient.

'Window-sill dead,' he decided, proud of having remembered.

'Window-sill dead! Whatever does he mean?' Virginia racked her brain. What complicated line of thought was he following? She had told him that the flowers were beautiful because he liked to look at them, and he answered, 'Window-sill dead'!

Why, of course! It must mean that he had realised the contrast between the living flowers, which were beautiful, and the deadness of the bare, white wood on which they were standing. He liked one and not the other. Only, of course, he didn't know the word for 'ugly.' She was delighted.

'Splendid, darling! But that's not quite right. Not "dead", but "ugly", we call things which are not beautiful. But Appius is perfectly right. The window-sill *is* ugly, and the flowers are beautiful. Good boy. Now look, there is beauty again.' She was pointing out of the window, across the garden, to where a red sunset was reflected in the clouds. 'Beauty,' she repeated. And then, pointing to the chrysanthemums, 'Beauty.' Appius stared at her, bewildered. She was not cross. His last answer must have been right. But this time he had no clue.

She helped him. 'Beauty,' she said, 'is what makes a thing beautiful. There is beauty in the flowers, and beauty in the sunset. Now say "beauty", darling. "Beauty."' She pronounced it slowly.

He understood now. That was what she wanted. A new word. It was a word and he must say it after her.

'Beauty,' he said after several attempts. She pointed to the flowers, and he repeated the word. Again to the sunset. 'What?' he added. But she was speaking again and didn't hear him.

'Now we'll have tea. Appius has been a good boy to-day. Put away the copy-book, and mama will fetch the tray.'

After tea she took him on her lap and talked to him. This had become a habit during the past week while he had seemed disinclined to work or play. It kept him from thinking too much, Virginia considered, and prevented his getting into mischief. Besides, listening to her was so good for him. It enlarged his vocabulary and widened his horizon. It should bring them closer together too, his hearing tales of her childhood. He would learn to think of her as a separate being like himself instead of merely as mama who fed him and ordered his life. Didn't most children get into closer contact with their parents through hearing about the great games in the garden of the old house, and the day Uncle Joseph fell into the pond, and how Aunt Amy screamed when he dropped a tadpole down her neck, and how cross grandmamma was? Appius had no uncles or aunts. That was a pity, for they would have made those far-off times more real to him. But there was the day she had caught the spider in the middle of the sermon, and papa had pointed at her from right up in the pulpit, and mama had taken her out quickly and slapped her in the porch, and she hadn't had any cake for tea. That would amuse him.

How well she remembered. Those sunny summer mornings in the village church; the cold smell of the stone-paved aisle and the damp shut-up smell of the pew when she knelt with her nose pressed against it: wood blackened and shiny with age and chipped by prehistoric penknives. What had happened to them, those hands which had dared to carve right under papa's terrible eye and had braved his nervous throat-clearing before a public rebuke? It must have been very long ago, for the chipped surfaces were as black now as the rest of the wood and worn smooth by the action of countless devout elbows.

Outside the open door the porch made a black tunnel, and at its end there was a hot rectangle of green churchyard sloping down to the lane, broken here and there by a wreath of pink and white dahlias on a village mound or a granite monument to one of the local gentry.

Nothing passed in the lane during service, for the main road was a mile or so away and all the villagers were in church, the men in ill-fitting broadcloth and creaking boots, their wives in sequined pelisses, which smelt of cupboard as they rustled past the rectory pew, and black bonnets with here and there a red rose bobbing up against a black memorial slab. Their daughters wore hats and stiff white muslin.

No sound broke the droning of her father's voice except the bleating of a sheep now and then and the distant hum of a threshing machine from Farmer Nelson's fields. He was the village atheist, and threshed loudest when parson was preaching. When Virginia went for a walk with her nurse they were careful to skirt Nelson's land. Even the village children avoided it, in the mushroom and blackberry seasons, for if Nelson caught a child gathering he would empty out its baskets and send it home crying. That was because he was a wicked man and didn't believe in God.

Virginia dreamt aloud, smiling absently at Appius, now and then giving him a laughing jig on her knee when his attention seemed to be wandering.

For some reason, she thought in one of these pauses, it was so much easier to talk to him since the upheaval the other day. Perhaps it was because her reserve had been broken down on that night she had been so tired. Perhaps it was because Appius had seemed to be older and steadier since that had happened. He was growing up, after all, and was naturally less interested in childish games and more inclined to listen sympathetically to her little confidences. She seized his face in her hands and kissed it.

Appius jumped. He had been drifting in a delightful world of warmth and softness, pillowed against mama's shoulder, with the fire glowing on his neck. Sometimes mama would bring him back with a jolt, but he had discovered that this only happened when his eyelids fell together; and he had found, too, that when he wasn't very sleepy, but only nicely, it was quite easy to keep them apart and drift away all the same; so long as he heard his name when she said it, and were ready to answer.

Chapter Twenty-Four

Virginia was laughing, a little tinkling laugh, looking at a picture in the book on her knee. After a moment she passed it to Appius in his deck-chair beside hers.

'Look, darling, what a funny picture. Doesn't Appius think it's funny?' She glanced sideways at him, rather anxiously, while he examined the book.

More than two years had passed since the question of his humanity had been raised and settled for good. It was summer again, the summer of his tenth year. At a few paces from his chair the lawn on which he had learnt to walk lay basking in the sun, its high grass white with ox-eye daisies and cuckooflowers, like a field up for hay. At its edge, where a narrow border had separated it from the path, tall madonna lilies still pushed up bravely between clumps of seeded grass and the weeds which had grown a little beyond Virginia's control. Red rambler roses hung in a heavy screen from the verandah roof and dragged at the pillars. The air was thick with heat.

Yes, Virginia thought, that crisis was long past. It seemed

to have faded from his memory, leaving him staider and less self-assertive than before. For her it stood out as a milestone in the path of his development, marking off the first stage of his childhood, his enthusiasm for history and 'great men' and digging, and ushering in a new epoch, an older and more sedate Appius, a closer companionship.

They had discovered the perfect relationship, she reflected now, glancing at his heavy features bent gravely above the volume she had given him. They were not only mother and son; they were friends. Appius enjoyed listening to her early reminiscences; he liked to sit quietly beside her, his hand clasped in hers; yet he would trot off obediently to play when she wanted to be alone. He was ready to talk or be silent according to her mood. But so far she had never been able to make him understand a joke.

That was possibly, she thought, because those she had shown him in the children's annuals on the nursery shelves had not appealed to him. Now she had unearthed some old bound volumes of *Punch* which had delighted her, she remembered, when she had discovered them, forty years before, in her father's library.

These should do excellently. She had brought them out here on to the verandah and carefully gone through them, choosing the simplest jokes and those most likely to appeal to a child's mind. Nothing political, of course, delightful though many of them were. The cartoons, now: not exactly humorous, of course, but she remembered her poor father's admiration for them.

She turned the volume on her knee.

Here was one which he had found particularly moving: one of the year '57, the Mutiny year, showing the old queen, in a group of her widowed subjects, calling down destruction on the wicked Indians. So touching, the sturdy figure in widow's weeds, her face glowing with righteous hatred; just as if Albert himself had been killed in the Black Hole, poor fellow, and of course he hadn't...

That had been long before Virginia's time, the Mutiny, but she remembered so well her father's showing her the old volumes, bemoaning the modern decline in wit. Still, he had had the contemporary numbers bound, and she had to confess that reviewing them now she found the later volumes scarcely less good than the earlier. So different, both of them, from the vulgar modern jokes: nothing in them at all. Poor dear father had naturally been a little biased in favour of the jokes of his youth, but in choosing examples for Appius she had been quite impartial, basing her choice upon the likely limits of his understanding.

She turned again and saw him conscientiously scanning the page she had pointed out to him.

'You see, darling? The old man has stepped on a banana skin and fallen down. Look at him with all his parcels and his umbrella flown all over the place. And there's the banana skin, you see—but he doesn't see it because it's behind him, and he's wondering why he has fallen. Isn't that funny, now?' She laughed her little tinkling laugh, but Appius seemed to be unmoved.

She would not let herself feel disappointed. Perhaps even that was not simple enough to begin with. Taking the volume from him, she ran through it to find the pages she had marked.

The crinoline jokes, now. He would hardly understand those. And the gentlemen in frock-coats who pulled at their moustaches and said 'Egad' and 'Damme, sir'; those wouldn't do either. Some of the child ones, perhaps, later. Then there were other gentlemen trying to find their way home and going round and round the railings of a square. But Appius couldn't be expected to understand drunkenness or appreciate its humour.

Finally there was the red-nosed group. Drunkenness again, of course, but he might see the humour of a man's having a red nose, even without knowing its cause. It was the incongruity of the thing: she remembered having read that this was the main occasion of laughter. That was what she must try to make him see.

She hesitated for a moment. Might these jokes recall the old trouble about the nature and appearance of man? Surely not, after more than two years. Although the word 'man' had scarcely been mentioned between them during that time, and the word 'ape' never, and he now invariably referred to himself as 'Appius' unqualified, he seemed to have accepted her explanations without further question and once or twice had even chanced upon pictures of 'great men' without showing emotion. It was essential now that he should look at these and learn to join her in appreciating a joke.

She chose a picture and passed it to him across the space separating their chairs.

'Now look carefully, darling, and mama will explain why it's funny.' She waited while he gripped the heavy volume firmly in his long thin hands. 'You see this man? He's got a red nose. Now you know that people don't have red noses, do they?'

Appius considered, examining the page and then her face. Her nose was pointed and yellowish.

'Nose red?' he said, puzzled.

'Yes. Nose red. Now because people don't have red noses as a rule, when someone does have a red nose we laugh. That means that we make a noise like this.' She tinkled again, then, to help him, enunciated clearly: 'Ha-ha.'

Appius watched her. So that was the meaning of the noise. It meant that someone had a red nose. Ha-ha. That was it. Nose red. Ha-ha.

'Ha-ha,' he said gravely.

Virginia beamed at him and laughed again.

'Dear child, how clever he is. Yes, that's right. Now we'll look at another picture.' She turned the page.

'Ha-ha,' said Appius, watching her face closely.

She looked up from the picture.

'Good boy. That's splendid. Now he can enjoy a joke with mama, can't he?'

'Ha-ha,' he answered.

She smiled and lifted the heavy volume from his knees.

'Now take mama for a walk.' She got up and drew his hand through her arm. He had grown a lot in the past two years; his head reached her shoulder now. Soon, she thought, he will be as tall as I am.

She glanced fondly at him as he strolled along at her side, clinging heavily to her arm. His figure had grown heavier lately, she noticed, and his face sterner. It had more character in it. The hair on his neck had not disappeared, as once she had hoped it might; indeed, it seemed to become thicker and longer as he grew. But it was not a disfigurement. She wondered why she had ever thought it so, ever wished that it should go. It gave him a strong, virile appearance and suited his heavy build, set off his broad, pink features. It was a good thing he had no hair on his face. She had never cared to see a man with a moustache or beard. Her father had been clean shaven.

They walked slowly, stopping now and then for Virginia to remove a sweet-pea pod or a faded rose bloom from the outer border, uninvaded by the lawn. Although she had aged a little in these last years and felt less inclined for heavy work, she had lost scarcely any of her briskness or interest in the garden.

Appius walked quietly at her side, his eyes bent for the most part on the ground a few paces ahead of him, but looking up to answer when she spoke.

He was a quiet child, she thought again, a quiet, serious child. But that was all the better. What would she have done if he had wanted always to be rushing about and taking violent exercise, or if he had grown impatient of their quiet way of life and fretted to leave her as he grew older?

'Here's a bush that wants tying up,' she remarked, stopping short. 'It's growing over on one side.'

'Bush want tying,' Appius agreed, stopping obediently.

Virginia was groping for the stem under the overhanging branches when her hand struck something hard on the ground.

'Why, it's the spade,' she exclaimed, dragging it out. She straightened herself, a little flushed from the scramble under the branches. 'It must have been here for years; it's quite rusty. I was wondering what had happened to it. Doesn't Appius want to play with it?'

Appius stared blankly.

'Spade?' he said uncertainly. He had dismissed it from his mind.

'Yes, the spade. Appius used to dig with it often, when he was a little fellow.'

She saw that he looked blank. After all, children's memories were short. She had a tendency sometimes to think him older than he really was. He looked more than his age.

'He's too old to play with it now, I expect,' she said brightly. Better not to bother him if he had forgotten about it. 'We'll take it into the house and clean it some time on a wet day. Come along. Mama must get some bass to tie up the bush.

Will Appius carry the spade?'

He took it from her uninterestedly and trailed it behind him as they went towards the house, his other hand drawn through Virginia's arm.

On the way she noticed an unusually large clump of groundsel in a prominent position among the rose bushes. Since Appius had stopped digging there had been nothing to keep the weeds down, she thought. Although she spent an evening at it now and then the garden was growing untidy. She took the spade from his hand and jerked at the groundsel, but the spade slipped and chopped through the stem.

'Mama is no good at digging, you see.' She tossed the weed over the wall, laughing at her failure.

Appius looked up and answered thoughtfully.

'Ha-ha,' he agreed.

She patted his hand and laughed again.

206

Chapter Twenty-Five

Appius was alone in the nursery. It was evening. He sat in the half-circle of light thrown by the fire and waited while mama drew the blinds downstairs and locked the door into the garden. Then she would come and talk to him.

He went to bed later now. Regularly, in the evenings, when Virginia's work was done, they would sit for an hour or so facing one another across the hearthrug while she told him for the hundredth time stories of her childhood and the days when she had lived in London, which was a big town where there were lots of houses close together and people living in all of them. He didn't understand most of what she said, but he liked the hum of her voice and the quietness of the warm room lit only by the fire and a reading-lamp on the table beside Virginia. It threw a circle of light around her which did not reach Appius. It made him more secure in the shadow at the far side of the rug where he sat with his hands on his knees in his own little armchair which had been ordered from London because he was too heavy now for mama's lap. While she talked he was able to watch her face moving, out there in the light, or shut his eyes and think about warmth and darkness and big moving shadows.

'Mama not come.'

She was late to-night. He got up and strode about the room, making the window-frames rattle. His hands were deep in his pockets and his heavy jowl was thrust forwards so that he could see the stretch of carpet lessening in front of him.

'Appius walk,' he muttered, turning at the fireplace. In half a dozen strides he had reached the opposite wall. 'Appius big, room small,' he noticed. He turned again, up and down, a dozen times.

'Appius cold. Appius go fire.' He stopped to warm his hands. 'Appius like fire.'

Suddenly he turned. 'Appius walk.' He strode up and down until he was giddy from the frequent turns.

'Why mama not come?' Then he heard her on the stairs, and stood still by the fire, waiting.

Virginia opened the door and stood holding it, pushing a strand of hair back from her eyes. She was flushed.

'Mama can't shut the hall window, darling. The damp must have made it stick again. Come and help mama, there's a good boy.'

He followed her downstairs. It was not the first time she had called him to help her when a window had stuck or there was something heavy to be moved. He put his hands under the sash and pushed.

'Thank you, darling.' She lowered the bottom sash and fastened the catch, smiling at him. 'What a blessing for mama that she has a big boy to do things for her. What would she do, now, if she were alone? Now we'll go upstairs and make ourselves cosy by the fire. Appius mustn't get cold.'

Back in the nursery she poked the fire and put on some more coal. Appius was already settled in his chair, leaning back in his favourite position: feet planted wide apart and hands dropped loosely on his knees.

She glanced at him sideways as she put down the poker. She wished sometimes that he would talk to her more openly, tell her more about himself. It was nice to have him so ready to listen, but he must have plenty to tell her if he chose and were not so reserved. It would be interesting to know what he thought about when he was alone, and what he could remember of his early impressions. Those race memories, now. Couldn't he recapture more than an ordinary child? He should, for he was closer to nature, after all. And could he remember what he used to think about when he was very small, before she had taught him to think in words?

She settled back into her chair.

'Well, darling,' she began briskly, taking her knitting from its bag. 'Mama has told Appius lots about herself. Now suppose Appius tells mama something about Appius.'

She paused, looking up encouragingly, but Appius was blank.

'Tell mama about Appius,' she coaxed.

'Appius.' He thought a long time. 'Appius warm,' he said at last.

'Yes, darling, and what else?'

He considered. What did mama want now? Why didn't she talk? Appius must talk. Why? Talk about Appius. Appius.

'Appius big,' he decided.

'Yes, dear.' He didn't understand what she wanted, of course. But this had given her something to go upon. 'But when Appius was small? Can he remember anything that happened when he was small?'

209

He frowned. Appius small? Why couldn't she go on talking and leave him alone?

'Appius not small. Appius big.'

'Yes.' She would be patient. 'Now Appius is big, but once he was small. Once he was only so high.' She held her hand a foot or two from the floor. 'First Appius small. Now Appius big.' She looked across at him questioningly.

'Appius small,' he agreed, and frowned thoughtfully. 'Now Appius big.'

'Now when Appius was small what did he do?'

'Appius do lessons. Appius go bed. Appius play garden.' He relapsed.

'That's right, but Appius wasn't very small then. Now what is the very first thing Appius can remember?'

Slowly he took in her meaning. Appius small, what?

'Mama,' he said at last.

Mama. There had always been mama. Mama feeding him, putting him to bed; mama showing him how to play, teaching him, dressing him, patting his head, talking to him. There was nothing before mama. 'Mama' must be right. He dropped the thought, satisfied with its conclusion, and drifted again.

Virginia smiled gently. Naturally she was the first thing he could remember. That was as it should be. She had never left him for a moment when he was small, except when he was asleep. It was only natural that she should have first place in his childish memories. Wasn't his mother every child's first impression? And how moving to hear him express it like this, so simply, 'Mama.' Just like that, in such a tone of certainty: the one thing which had been vivid to his child's consciousness. But what of that other, older consciousness? He must have had dreams, dreams of the jungle, perhaps; some relic of the life of his ancestors since the beginning of time. She would try him again.

'Tell mama, darling.' Her voice was soft and caressing. 'Does Appius ever have dreams? Does he remember dreaming when he was very small? Does Appius ever see things when he's asleep?'

With a jerk Appius came back to the fireside.

Why couldn't she leave him alone? She had been quiet just long enough for him to drift away. He had been lying among the leaves, so soft: big, padded leaves, swaying very gently, fanning him.

Now he was back in his chair, sitting upright with his feet on the carpet.

'Appius asleep see things?' He frowned quite angrily. Stupid. Sleep meant darkness, seeing nothing. 'See things' meant light, things around him: mama, chair, fire, table. But he must answer her so that she would stop asking. 'Appius asleep not see things.'

'Nothing at all?' She was surprised. Now what might he have seen? The jungle. Trees, perhaps. 'When Appius was small, can he remember seeing trees, ever?'

Trees. He thought a long time. Trees. Garden. Appius not like trees. He knew that, although he didn't know why.

'Appius not like trees,' he muttered sulkily.

Virginia sighed.

'Very well, darling. We won't talk about trees any more if Appius doesn't like them.' She took up the knitting which she had dropped on to her lap.

It was a little disappointing, she thought, but perhaps gradually she might help him to remember. Perhaps after all it was a good sign, that dislike of trees. It might mean that he had had intuitions when he was small and now subconsciously rejected them as belonging to a way of life he had put aside.

Perhaps he had had visions which had frightened him at the time although he had forgotten them now. Those fear dreams of childhood. If terrifying memories persisted in children after thousands of centuries of civilisation, how much more might they in him. Perhaps later he would be able to tell her.

For a few moments Appius watched her finger sliding rhythmically backwards and forwards, drawing the wool. Her face was lowered over the work and she was quiet again. He slipped back among the leaves.

They sat in silence until bedtime.

Chapter Twenty-Six

Virginia was sitting at her writing-table, in the corner by the nursery fire, tapping its wood with her pen.

It was Appius's tenth birthday; that is to say, the tenth anniversary of his coming to the cottage, for this was the day which Virginia had always observed as a festival. That other, rather earlier, date she did not care to dwell upon; it suggested an impudent infringement of her maternal rights in Appius. That there was probably in existence somewhere even at that moment a shaggy female orang-utan... Virginia shuddered and turned her papers quickly.

Here was the diary in which she had continued to enter particulars of Appius's growth and mental development for some years after the record book supplied by the infants' food manufacturer had been completed. She turned the leaves meditatively. Here was her entry made when he first spoke, when he first walked. Here was the day he began to read; the day he fell out of the tree; the day he first talked of his own accord. Here was the time the policeman came, after the children had been on the wall.

She sighed. What colossal difficulties there had been in those ten years. Yet somehow they had been overcome. There had been times when everything had seemed to go wrong; when it had seemed that she couldn't possibly go on; yet she had gone on, and reached success at last. She flushed proudly as she turned the leaves.

There had been times when under the stress of circumstances the entries had ceased altogether; when, for instance, he had caught a feverish cold and she had watched him day and night, afraid of some development she could not foresee.

Memory filled in the gaps.

There was the time he had cut his foot with the spade and she had had to keep him indoors, with the bandaged foot on a chair, and fight for days against his fretful boredom. There were the times he had lost his appetite and refused to eat the nourishing vegetables and rice she cooked for him; that day he had thrown his porridge about the room and would eat nothing but a little fruit, and she had been at her wits' end. And then there was the time he had discovered that originally he had not been a man.

What a terrible crisis that had been. But even that had been passed, with infinite patience and tact.

Then lately, in the past two years, there had been little to record. There had been a steady progression towards mutual understanding and companionship.

In those early years how desperately tired she had been, sometimes; worn to a shadow of herself, and she had never been really strong, either. It was wonderful, really, what she had managed to do. She had aged, she knew, during those ten years. Her hair had grown thinner and began to be white over the ears; her cheeks were more hollow; she had to stop to get her breath after running upstairs.

But hadn't it been abundantly worthwhile? She might be getting old, but she had a son who would be a real companion to her in her old age; who was quiet and thoughtful and sprang to help her with his strength and kept her company through the long evenings.

He was growing up fast. He was ten to-day. Only ten, it was true, but far older and steadier than she had imagined a child of his age could be. And he would grow still more in understanding as time went on. The troublesome part of his childhood was over and she was beginning to reap the benefit of her work. Perhaps some day they would even be able to travel together. She was not old yet. She was not quite fifty. There was plenty of time. And then, when she got really old, they would settle down again, contented and self-sufficing in their seclusion as they were now.

She shuffled the pages.

She had thought at one time that he might go to the university when he grew up, but she had rather dropped that idea lately. And he had never had the tutor to prepare him for school. Never mind. She was able to teach him herself; she would be able to teach him more and more as he grew. Why, she could give him practically a university education herself. She would look out the notes she had taken as a student— they must be somewhere about—and rub up subjects in which she had got rusty, by the time he was ready for them. Besides, he might go to a university even yet. Abroad, perhaps. That question of his origin would matter less among foreigners…

How much they had gained, though, Appius and she, by not having a tutor. They would hardly have reached such a pitch of intimacy and comradeship with a third person in the house for the last two or three years.

A folded paper fluttered from between the leaves she was

215

turning. 'Evolution Theory: Explanation Given to Appius.' Ah. She had meant to elaborate upon that and perhaps publish it some day.

She glanced down the headings: Origin of man; Brain the only distinction; Relation to and explanation of the Eden Myth.

'The curse of man is his brain.' How true that was, she thought. All the misery of man, the revenge taken by nature for his obstinacy and pride in acquiring that which other animals could do without. Revenge taken through the brain itself, which tormented him with useless and ridiculous scruples, and through the body which was never meant to contain a brain and in so doing had become liable to diseases and disorders unknown to other creatures.

The curse of woman, too, she thought; for didn't the curse of Eve fall more heavily in proportion to brain development? She flushed a little. In her day biology lectures for women students had been scrupulously censored.

...And the torments of the brain itself. She swung back quickly to her previous idea. 'The moral law within man.' Could this be other than a parasitical growth; the offshoot of a primitive conceit which, not content with one world and a body, must invent a soul and a world to come? How pathetic if this were so.

She mustn't forget that. She must add a note to the memorandum while she remembered.

'So we see...' She hesitated, her pen hovering above the paper. How should it go? Never mind, it could be worked up later. She must put down the important part before she forgot it. '... All the ideals, the strivings, the ethical principles, the heavenward aspirations of man, nothing but the curiosity of an ape wading towards the edge of a deep primaeval forest.'

She put down her pen and read, pleased with what she had written. She must remember to work this up into an article, or perhaps into a chapter of her book on the experiment when she had collected and arranged all the data. It was a pity she had not taken notes consistently. How was it? She had been too busy, she supposed; too much occupied with the living Appius to care for him simply as the subject of her experiment. She had meant to publish notes on its progress years ago.

Well... Her sigh changed to a smile as she heard Appius coming in from the garden. He was her own big boy. Nobody but she herself had had the tiniest part in his upbringing. He was her very own, and she had him with her for always.

She bundled her notes into a drawer and got up as he came in.

'Why, mama's own darling boy! He's stayed out late to-day. Look, it's beginning to get dark.'

'Appius walk,' he explained.

'Come along, then. He can warm himself by the fire while mama gets his birthday tea.' She fussed about him, taking off his coat, drawing his chair closer to the fire, piling coal on to the red embers.

When she had gone downstairs Appius did not sit down. He walked up and down the room, muttering: 'Appius walk. Appius want tea.' He went round and round. There was more room that way than straight up the middle and back again.

'Appius cold.' That brought him to the hearth where the fire was slowly reviving, and just then Virginia came in with the tea, and his birthday cake alight with ten candles.

'There. Just look. A cake all for Appius because it's his birthday.' She set the tray down and poked the fire until the flames rose again, so that they could have tea by its light.

Appius was examining the cake.

'Appius?' he asked.

'Yes, all for Appius. Appius's birthday cake.'

'Appius.' He felt it all round, pleased with his ownership. 'Appius like cake.'

She was repaid for the hours she had spent in the kitchen, one morning, before he was awake.

Carefully she extinguished one candle and cut him a slice. The icing was hard, but he ate it with gusto because it was his. It had been a long time since he had had a cake of his very own. He remembered only vaguely that there had been cakes like this before and that they had had candles, too.

Virginia was smiling at him. 'Appius needn't do any lessons this evening because it's his birthday,' she said when he had finished. 'He can sit in his little chair and talk to mama instead.' She pushed back the table and drew their chairs closer to the fire.

'Now,' she said, when he was seated facing her. 'Does Appius know what day it is to-day? Does he know why he did no lessons this morning and none this evening, and why he had a cake of his very own, with candles on it, for tea? That's because it's his birthday.'

'Birthday what?' She had waited for him to say something.

'Birthday is the day Appius was born.' She corrected herself quickly: 'The day Appius came to live with mama, ten whole years ago.'

He said nothing.

'You understand, darling? To-day Appius has lived with mama for ten whole years. Now you know what a year is. It's the time since Appius had a birthday cake before; and there have been ten of them since Appius began living with mama.'

Appius wrinkled his brow. What was mama saying? Appius, mama, ten cakes? What did she want him to say? 'Appius like

218

cake'?

But as he was opening his mouth she spoke again. 'Doesn't Appius like living with mama? Isn't he glad that he came to live with her?' She sighed momentarily. She wished sometimes that he would be a little quicker to respond. 'Doesn't Appius like mama?'

So that was it.

'Appius like mama.'

He hadn't thought about it before. It hadn't occurred to him that mama was a thing for Appius to like or not, like cake, or playing in the garden, or arithmetic. She was just there. But that was right: 'Appius like mama,' not 'Appius like cake.' That was what she had wanted, because she was pleased now, smiling and leaning forwards to pat his knee.

He repeated it: 'Appius like mama.'

She leant back and beamed at him.

'Darling boy. Of course Appius likes mama. But he can't like mama half so much as mama likes Appius, because she's watched him grow, and looked after him for years and years before he noticed her at all. Appius can never know how mama has loved him and cared for him all this time.'

She felt herself enwrapped in a warm mist of sentiment; affection for him mingling with a retrospective affection and pity for her own earlier self, that self which had struggled and been alone and finally won happiness from a hostile world.

Appius sat watching her and wondering why her voice was wobbly and soft, not clear and brisk as usual, nor quiet and smoothly flowing as it was when she strayed off upon some childish memory. He thought it was queer. And she was pinker than usual, too. As a rule she was whitish or pale yellow.

Now she was bending forwards again, stretching out her hand towards him. What did she want? But she was only talking.

'Darling child,' Virginia said, 'you can't know how lonely mama was before she had you. She didn't even have the cottage to live in alone. She lived in a room in a big town where millions and millions of other people live in rooms all alone. But she wasn't with them. Some of them came and talked to her, but they weren't like Appius. They didn't like mama. They laughed at her and went away again and said she was mad because she was interested in other things besides shopping and gossiping with them. And then when she'd found Appius they said more than ever that she was mad, just because she was happy at last. Nobody ever liked mama until Appius came.' Her voice was rising, high and thin.

Appius stared at her from under his brows. She was so queer this evening that he couldn't drift away and forget she was there as he usually did. Besides, he didn't want to drift away. He wanted to get up and walk and walk. He felt wide awake, and alive all over; not a bit drowsy. He wished he could get up and walk. But he couldn't because mama was looking at him all the time. She had dropped her knitting on to the floor and seemed to have forgotten about it. Why did she keep bending towards him, too, when her voice rose, so that he had to listen, and then dropping back again into the chair and talking on and on so quickly? He was uneasy. His ears twitched. Why couldn't he get up and walk round and round? He couldn't keep still much longer.

Mama was talking on and on, her voice rising and falling suddenly in unexpected places. Gradually it was rising higher and for longer at a time. He *must* keep still. Mama would be cross if he got up. But every bit of him wanted to move, was creeping by itself, under his skin, as he wouldn't move it. He fidgeted with his hands on his knees and twisted his feet about, toes in and then the heels as far as they would go, carefully, so that she wouldn't notice.

Virginia was leaning forwards again, further than ever. Her voice rose in a wail. She was melting in self-pity.

'Nobody, nobody but Appius ever liked mama. Nobody ever. You can't understand what it is, always to be alone. You can't have any idea.

'Appius, my own darling child, you do love mama a little, don't you? Just a little. Say you do. Tell mama you do. Mama has nobody but you.'

Appius was fidgeting frantically. He couldn't keep still. What was the matter with mama? She couldn't keep still, either. Her words had no meaning for him, but her tone exasperated him, goading him into movement. His ears were burning, and he could feel his throat beginning to work.

Mama was flinging out both her hands towards him now, calling him. Now she had thrown herself back into the chair again and was lying there, quiet for a moment.

Appius gasped, choking. A hot tide was rising swiftly through him. Not only his ears but the whole of him was burning now. What was it? What was the matter? Why was mama crying like that and talking at the same time? Why were her eyes so bright and shiny?

What was this that was happening to him?

Then something leapt in him: something leaping, and urging him outwards from the chair, from himself. Himself pushing outwards from himself.

He tried to think. Must be still. Mama be cross. But the tide drowned his thoughts. He felt his throat contract and dilate; heard a rumble. In a moment he was upon her and she was falling backwards, screaming weakly.

She shrank, struggling, leaning as far as she could over the arm of the chair. Then she lay still and closed her eyes. She thought: he may kill me. He may not. All her strength was gone.

Suddenly it returned. Feverishly she knocked against his shoulders with both hands, but he was too strong for her. Then the habit of years pushed its way upwards through her numbed brain. She raised her head and stared at him with cold fury.

'Appius.'

She repeated it twice. Slowly the habit of a lifetime pierced the red mist which was blinding him. His hands loosened. He slid from the chair and slunk to the far side of the room, into the shadow.

She couldn't repeat the effort.

Without knowing how, she had got through the door and shut it behind her and reached her own room and turned the key.

Chapter Twenty-Seven

Appius strode up and down the nursery faster and faster, upsetting whatever came in his way. His desk crashed, and his chair. The table heaved over and then righted itself leaving the tea-tray and cake upside down on the floor. Appius strode over them, grinding china and sugar-icing into the carpet.

Habit had sobered him only for a moment. He swung backwards and forwards, taking the room in three strides, in two; arms swinging, head bent, mumbling to himself. He had no thoughts. The mist had smothered them, the tide had drowned them. He had no thoughts, but he felt; and all he felt was the rush and surge of the tide.

Objects struck him. He seized and swung them and heard them crash.

One bound. He was almost across the room. Another, and he had hurled himself heavily against the wall. He struck it with his fists, but it would not give way. He raged round and round, at last finding the door.

There was space in the passage. He strode along it and half

fell down the stairs. In the hall the blind had not been drawn, and a full moon was shining brilliantly over the tiled floor.

Appius lunged backwards and forwards, overturning the centre table. He fell against a chair and sat heavily on it, puffing out his mouth in an effort to breathe. From there he could see the moon shining full upon him.

He heaved himself out of the chair and shambled over to the window. He stared full at the moon, and his mouth writhed at it. Flecks of foam shaken from his lips plopped virulently against the pane and meekly slid, dissolving, down its shiny surface.

Waves roared and surged around him, buffeting him. Darkness roared, torn by jagged streams of light.

The tide swelled, swifter and more swift. A whirlpool of darkness raced around him, around and around. Streaks of light flashed through it, faster and more fast: zigzags swelling and curving in a frenzy of speed until they joined and so sped onwards, rising and coiling around him and around, a spiral of flame which singed the hissing waves.

He clutched the sill and stood swaying and snarling, half hanging by his hands. He was giddy, dazed by the swirl and dazzle of flame and tide, gripped the sill and staggered in the moaning waters. Abruptly the darkness was torn in front of him and into the rent came the moon, riding unperturbed in a pale sky.

He snarled. This chill, white globe was, he sensed in some obscure way, his tormentor: it was this which had sent the darkness and the waters to engulf him.

Standing erect, he threw his head backwards and thumped his chest with his powerful fist and spoke.

'Appius! *Man*!'

Defiance, hatred, fear were flung, jangled together, full in the moon's face. Then he fell on to all-fours and, raising his head, barked many times the hoarse short bark of the jungle ape at full moon.

The moon shone dispassionately.

Appius rushed howling across the hall. Red mist blinded him. With his hands he groped for the stairs. Fear of the unknown, the instinct to hide, habit which had no need of thought, sent him stumbling on hands and feet back to his own lair, back to the nursery.

Chapter Twenty-Eight

Virginia sat very still on her bed. She had been sitting there ever since she had locked the door. She had no strength to move. She tried to think what could be done, but she could only think: How horrible. How terrible. How horrible.

She could hear Appius rushing about the nursery and the furniture being overturned.

How horrible, she thought. How terrible.

Then the nursery door burst open. He was coming. A cold hand closed over her heart. She could feel it beating against the fingers. She was choking.

But he had gone by. Of course, the door was locked.

How horrible. What should she do? There was nothing to do. Stay here and die. Go out and let him kill her.

He may recover, she thought. He's been like this before. He was almost as bad when he saw himself in the mirror.

But not quite, she thought. That was different. There was something different to-day. What was it? What had she done? What was the matter with him? There was something horrible about him. What was it? What could she do?

He was in the hall now, throwing things about. Supposing he broke out and got away. Well, he would have gone. If he went on like this, what was to happen?

It was terrible, she thought. Terrible. It wasn't only he himself. 'He seemed to have taken all my strength from me. I had no will to defend myself. I believe I should have let him kill me. Why didn't I? What happened?

'Now I must do something about it. What can I do?'

She stood up, but her knees gave way and she sat down again without noticing that she had done so.

It was as if he had gone mad. He must have gone mad. It was different from all the other times. Quite different. He will kill me.

Unless I kill him.

The thought struck her suddenly like a stone. She gasped. She had not thought it. It had come from somewhere outside her and fallen, fully voiced, on her brain.

The pistol. Father's pistol. It couldn't be loaded, though.

Why not? He used to keep it in his study drawer in case of burglars. It's in the trunk with his things. I saw it when I was looking for the globe for Appius.

She shivered.

How horrible.

Crawling from the bed, she knelt beside the trunk and raised its creaking lid. She rummaged. There was the old clock that used to stand in his study. She lifted it out and stood it on the floor. It began to tick, a hollow tick which had been long dead, and then stopped. The room was very still.

There was the pistol. She took it from its case and examined it cautiously. Yes, it was loaded. Father must have loaded it years before he died. It must have been loaded for twenty years at least. It would hardly go off now. She put it on the floor, replaced the clock and shut the trunk.

Then she heard Appius shout in the hall. He was coming upstairs. Again fear strangled her. She knelt, clutching the trunk, not breathing. When he had passed, and slammed the nursery door, she found that she had taken up the pistol and was grasping it in her right hand. She dropped it slowly.

But I can't kill him, she thought. He's my child.

I can't kill him.

From somewhere in the distance she heard herself answer: Nonsense. You know he's not your child. You know he's an ape. He will kill you if he gets the chance. You must kill him.

She shrank, gripping the trunk with both hands.

I can't. It isn't true. He's my child. He's all I've got. I can't, I won't kill him.

You must, she said.

I can't. He's mine. My child. I can't kill my child. Murder. I can't murder my child.

Murder? Your child? A monstrosity you've raised up. The child of your diseased brain. A thing which should never have lived; which but for you would not have existed. You've made it. You must kill it.

I can't, she said. I can't.

She lay, half stretched out on the floor, her arms thrown across the trunk and her head resting on them.

After a time she moved. Had she been unconscious? It must be very late.

Her glance wandered idly over the floor. There was something white under the wardrobe. Something quite large. She must see what it was. Crawling on hands and knees, she reached underneath and pulled out a tattered book. The Animal Alphabet. How did it get there? She brought it back to the trunk and fluttered the pages.

A for Ape. Of course. That day he had gone mad and broken the mirror. It had never been mended. He must have found this in the nursery bookshelf. It must have been there all the time. She had never bothered to look through all the books.

So it was my fault, that. It must have unhinged his mind. That's why he has gone mad now. Only this is different. So that is why I must kill him. I've killed him already.

Weak tears were oozing from her eyes. She lay quietly against the trunk, her face uncontorted, and felt their zigzag paths over her cheek-bones and watched them drip on to the alphabet. She was too much exhausted to cry violently or to dry the tears.

The carpet smelt dusty. It wanted beating. No carpets had been taken up since the cottage was furnished. That was ten years ago. But if she had a man in, Appius would kill him.

She lay there thinking: supposing he killed me. What would happen to him? He would be hanged. No. They wouldn't know he was my son. They'd treat him as an animal. But he's not an animal. He's my child. He can't live without me.

She drifted again, out beyond thought.

Suddenly she knew that there was no noise in the nursery. She must do it now, whilst he was asleep.

Slowly her hand felt over the carpet for the pistol. She crept along the passage; without a sound she opened the nursery door.

The light was still burning as she had left it. Furniture was overturned and broken china trampled into the carpet. Appius was lying asleep on the bed, outside the clothes. She crept over and stood by the foot of the bed, levelling the pistol at his heart.

Suddenly her knees gave way. Her strength was oozing,

pouring from her in an aching flood. She tottered alongside him, holding out her arms. The pistol dropped from her hand.

'Appius, my darling. I can't. Appius!' She fell on the bed, face downwards, beside him.

Appius woke and snarled. The red mist flared; the waves closed over his head.

Chapter Twenty-Nine

'**A**ppius hungry.'

He was prowling about the hall, muttering to himself: 'Appius hungry. Appius want breakfast.'

The dining-room door was unlocked, but the room stood empty and self-possessive, ignoring human needs. The waxed table with its centre bowl of pink autumn roses shone in the afternoon sunlight, two polished chair-tops diametrically protruding above its edge. The silver breakfast service was neatly arranged on the sideboard; uptilted tray supported in the centre by the teapot and on either side by sugar-bowl and milk-jug. There was nothing to eat.

Appius wandered out again into the hall and discovered the door near the stairs through which mama brought the tray at meal times. He explored, glancing around him uneasily. This part of the house was unfamiliar to him.

'Appius hungry,' he muttered, to give himself courage. 'Appius want breakfast.' He plodded across the kitchen.

The scullery felt damp. A steady drip-drip was coming from the tap over the sink and an uneven drip and rustle from the ivy beyond the barred window. Everything else was very quiet. He shivered and retreated quickly through the kitchen. There was no food lying about, and it did not occur to him to open cupboards.

Back in the dining-room he smashed the french window with his fist and crawled through on to the verandah. He shambled uneasily across the lawn, his feet making a squishing noise in the sodden turf under the rank, beaten grass. The lower part of his face was thrust forwards, mouth busily muttering. His eyes, very small and red, were almost hidden by his brows and shaggy tufts of hair. More and more acutely he was conscious of the hunger which was gnawing him.

'Appius hungry. Appius want breakfast.' He spoke with more decision as the bright autumn sunshine penetrated his torn jersey and reached his chilled skin. 'Appius hungry.'

But nothing took any notice of him. He crossed on to the path and plodded on, hands deep in pockets, between ranks of bare, indifferent bushes. A row of draggled, yellow daisies lurched alongside him. One here and there which was bending drunkenly over the wet stony soil flapped damply against his legs as he passed.

Suddenly he lifted his head and shouted: 'Mama! Appius hungry! Mama come!' There was no answer.

Then he remembered. Mama not come. Mama dead.

He stopped short in astonishment. It had not occurred to him before, this connection between mama and breakfast and the hump of purple wool which was huddled on his bed, upstairs in the nursery, and wouldn't move when he poked it.

Mama dead.

For a moment he stared about him, baffled. Then an idea struck him. Through the bare twigs at his side he could see something green and yellow: a bed of cabbages gone to seed.

Pushing his way through the wet, prickly bushes, he up-rooted the nearest cabbage and set off for the house with it firmly tucked under his arm, roots dangling, small yellow blooms gaily nodding.

He went straight to the nursery. The light was still burning and the blinds were drawn. It was cold. Appius looked at the grate, but it was choked with brownish grey ashes. He turned his back on it and crossed the room, avoiding the overturned furniture and crockery. He made for the bed.

Virginia was lying there, face downwards, her head dangling over the edge and one hand trailing limply on the carpet. As Appius gave her a push she slid from the bed and fell with a thud face upwards, on the floor, saying nothing.

Mama still dead.

Appius planked the cabbage firmly on her chest and drew back to admire the effect.

'Flowers,' he said proudly. Then he looked again, more closely, and frowned, trying to remember.

His face cleared. Standing astride her, he raised his head and pointed, triumphantly, downwards. With a shout he called the room to witness: 'Face blue. Ha-ha.'

THE END

Acknowledgements

The publishers would like to thank Brad Bigelow for his authoritative introduction and for all the fine work he does to highlight writers and books that have been forgotten, sidelined or ignored. We encourage you to visit his website, The Neglected Books Page.

neglectedbooks.com

Abandoned Bookshop

Abandoned Bookshop was founded in 2016 by Kat Stephen and Scott Pack. Its mission is to track down forgotten books of the past and re-publish them for a modern audience. Our authors include Nobel Prize-winning Italian novelist, Grazia Deledda, Norman Thomas di Giovanni, Jules Verne, Stein Riverton, George Barker, Palle Rosenkrantz and Clifton Robbins.

abandonedbookshop.com